Praise for *Collapse Years*

"If you're looking for a well-written post apocalypse with a wonderful collection of diverse characters and stories with depth, definitely come experience the fall of civilization with *Collapse Years*!"

— Joshua Grant
#1 bestselling author
Diabolic Shrimp CEO

"Damir Salkovic's polished prose [drew] me into a dark and desperate world that I couldn't put down."

— Scott Coon
Lost Helix

"A collection of stories about an agonizing dying world. *Collapse Years* has everything—compelling worlds, rich characters, pain and suffering. Damir Salkovic has poured his soul into this powerful book.

— Costi Gurgu,
Green Corrosion

"A provocative, resonant read...that will expand your mind about the journey our own world is venturing [toward and] will resonate with you for a long time."

— The Wulvers Library,
FanFiAddict

"Salkovic has an enviable talent for drawing readers in and keeping them hooked with quick pacing and potent characterisation.... A provocative, resonant read."

— Damien Lawardorn
Aurealis Magazine

Collapse Years

Opening Note

What you are about to read is a deeply personal work and intact expression of its author's exploration of the truth. For this reason, we strongly encourage you to explore all of the details and implications of anything you discover or encounter as a result of this work.

In accordance with The Mad Duck Coalition's mission of encouraging and providing intellectual stimulation of all kinds, we cannot endorse any of the ideas presented by any individual member of our flock.

The only things we endorse are the authorial integrity of the works we publish and the quality of intellectual engagements that they produce and inspire.

Collapse Years

By Damir Salkovic

Flights of Fancy

Ithaca, NY

2024 The Mad Duck Coalition ™ First Edition

THE MAD DUCK COALITION, its imprints, and colophones are trademarks of The Mad Duck Coalition, LLC.

For information about our special discounts for libraries, reviews, bookstores, and academic professionals, contact us through our form at thmaduco.org

Published in the United States under Flights of Fancy, an imprint of The Mad Duck Coalition, LLC, New York.

Cover art by Matthew Revert

Paperback: 978-1-956389-19-7
Hardback: 978-1-956389-21-0
Epub: 978-1-956389-20-3

Library of Congress Control Number: 2023951813

www.themadduckcoalition.org

To Bootsy (2006 - 2023)

Table of Contents

HANTU

Arjani was standing near the camp gate, watching the supply trucks roll in through sheets of rain, when she saw the *hantu* again.

The ghost looked like a winged dragon, about the size of a housecat. Radiant colors and iridescent scales, the apparition didn't seem to mind the mud or the drizzle. It pranced in the tall grass for a moment, tossed back its shaggy head, then vanished into the dripping trees.

Safe from the rain under the tin roof of the barracks, Arjani cupped her hands around her tea mug and inhaled the fragrance, watching the jungle for a flash of brightness, or the wag of an unrepentant tail. It was common knowledge that Tambak Eleven was haunted, but there was a difference between knowing it and seeing it for oneself. She propped herself on her toes, but the food convoy had decided to halt right in front of her, blocking her view.

Soldiers leaped off the backs of the vehicles, unloading sacks of rice and protein concentrate, their bare feet churning up the mud. Some old and weary-eyed, others looking like adolescent boys, thin necks and wrists sticking out of collars and sleeves. Rumor among the camp elders was that this last contingent had driven down all the way from the north, that the whole army was on the move, trying to stop the coast from sliding into the sea. Arjani giggled the first time she heard this, imagining men and women in uniform standing shoulder to shoulder in the frothing water, pushing back the sand and the jungle.

It's not a laughing matter, Bapak had chided her, worry written into the premature lines of his face. The government was in disarray, millions of desperate people fled their homes to avoid drowning, and the unfed, exhausted army was on the brink of mutiny. Once the soldiers abandoned this refugee camp, there would be nothing to eat. The lights would go out. Then where would the family go?

Home, Arjani wanted to say, but she knew better. Such a place no longer existed. The sea had clasped its hands over their island and pulled it down into its wet embrace. Not satisfied with this conquest, it continued to move inland, a few centimeters here and there at first, gradually growing bolder, until the monsoons caused the rivers to swell and overrun their banks. Arjani and her family had relocated to one of the government camps on the mainland, unclaimed, rootless. Unwanted. Their world was a huddle of dilapidated structures surrounded by a fence that served more as a symbol than a guarded perimeter. Those outside didn't want in. No one inside had anywhere to escape to.

The world is shaking, Mbah Sastri often told Arjani and her siblings, and any of the other camp children who happened to be around. *In its bowels, the serpent-dragon, the naga, is moving. Waking up from centuries of deep dreaming. The sea rages and its waves eat people's homes. When there is turmoil,* hantu *are released. Ghosts with one foot in this world and the other in the next.*

Arjani's thoughts quickly turned to hunger as she plodded across the camp's soft, waterlogged ground, her tea gone cold, the drizzle soaking into her shapeless uniform. She found her family in their usual corner of the dining hall, shoulder to shoulder with the other evacuees from the village: even this far from home, people gravitated to their own kind. "There you are," her mother said, her tone accusing. "We didn't think you'd grace us with your presence. We almost ate your portion too."

"I'm sorry, *ibu*," Arjani said to her mother, casting her eyes downward to show contrition, like a good daughter was supposed to. "I was at the gate. The convoy was late coming in. The roads are flooded. When the guards unloaded the rice, some of the grains were spoiled. I heard one of them say that. It made the other soldiers angry."

"Disease," her father said quickly, with a pointed glance at Mbah Sastri, who pretended not to notice, gnawing a lump of undercooked HiPro cake with her toothless mouth. "That rice is bad. Eating it would have made us sick."

"Why would the guards give us bad rice?" Arjani asked. She decided not to mention the dancing dragon: it would only get her deeper into trouble.

"Because they are liars," her mother said. Shook her head when Bapak clamped his hand over hers, silently imploring her to be quiet. "Because they take the good rice and fill their bellies with it. Or sell it. Then they put the poison into our pots and cook it. That's why there isn't enough food. Because the thieves and liars steal it. They only think of themselves."

"We don't know that's what happened," Bapak said, with a worried glance toward the guard at the entrance. "Maybe the rice was loaded already spoiled. We should not blame the soldiers for every little thing that goes wrong. Everyone is doing the best they can."

"Maybe it was the *hantu*." Mbah's eyes gleamed inside their nests of wrinkles. "Maybe it changed the rice inside the sacks. Eh! Magic is how they do it."

"Where are these *hantu* during the day?" Komang, the youngest child, wore a suspicious expression that pinched his thin face even thinner. "I've never seen one."

"Of course not." The old woman made a grand gesture, surreptitiously winking at Arjani. "You don't have the sight to see the unliving. But the *hantu* sees *you*. It creeps through the walls and sits there in the dark. Watching you sleep." Her wizened face loomed over the terrified boy, inching closer, like she was about to kiss him. "Then, when you least expect it to, the   will breathe into your mouth. Your body will be frozen, unable to move. That's when it steals your soul."

"Nonsense." Bapak shook his head. A slight, bespectacled man, a reserved optimist by nature, he maintained a blind faith in science as a tool of progress, a dogmatic approach to being open-minded. "There is no such thing as ghosts and goblins. Your grandmother should know better than to fill your heads with silly superstitions."

"Superstitions." Mbah Sastri sneered at her son. "I'll tell you what's superstitious. A man waving his degree at the sea, trying to order the waves to turn around. Your piece of paper against God's will. But I'm the superstitious one."

"*Hantu* have no need for rice," Ibu said in a waspish tone. "Fat, lazy bureaucrats are a different matter."

"Enough about the *hantu*." Bapak looked tired, ready to lay his head on the table and go to sleep. "The rice is spoiled because of a fungus spreading everywhere caused by the floods. It's affecting all crops. We all heard about it on the government broadcasts. That's why there's a famine. Not because of ghosts."

Arjani looked from face to face, taking in the dull eyes and worry lines. Her father had been his island's first coastal engineer and built a western-style house and planned bright futures for his children. Now just another one of life's castaways, his back no longer straight and his head bowed under an invisible weight. Ibu, her sharp schoolteacher's mind busy dividing the *sambal* and *goreng* between the hungry mouths in her household. Mbah Sastri, reduced to a barracks cot and handouts from a mobile kitchen in her old age. *Hantu*, all of them. No matter how daintily they picked at the steaming rice, or washed it down with sips of weak tea, pretending that they're at a banquet, they weren't fooling anyone. They were only going through the motions: they no longer belonged in this world. Any day now, she would blink, and they would disappear, like the island had disappeared, fading into memory.

"Little girl." The woman squatting outside the camp gate smiled a gapped smile at Arjani, beckoning her closer with gnarled hands, arms like mottled sticks, and a weathered face almost leathery from the sun. She picked through the pile of fruit on the tarp before her, held out two dark green objects. "Come take a look. They're good. Sweet."

It was fruit she had in her hands. The woman was one of the farmers from down below, from the flooded fields under the causeway. Several of them had gathered in front of the gate, offering fruit and vegetables and NexGen rice from jute sacks, squinting in the hot midday sun. They weren't supposed to take any plants out of the exclusion zone: everything that grew there had to be burned. But the most desperate did it anyway. The lone guard at the camp's gate either no longer bothered to chase them away or had been bribed somehow.

In spite of Bapak's warnings, Arjani felt her stomach clench painfully with hunger, her feet moving of their own accord. Almost overnight, the camp had emptied of soldiers, who had looted the food stores on their way out. If she walked through the gate, no one would stop her. The heat of the day seared through her hair, seeming to melt her thoughts. Her legs felt rubbery with hunger.

The farmer woman holding up the fruit grinned wider, more desperately. "Come, pretty girl. How long has it been since you've tasted a mango? I'll give you a good price."

Her hands, Arjani saw, were covered in flesh-colored gloves up to the elbows. Paler than the rest of her, the fingers dirty and frayed, revealing cracked nails. The woman beckoned again, holding out the succulent fruit.

Why wasn't anyone coming out to peruse the farmers' wares? Surely they had to be as hungry as Arjani felt. She could see them clustering inside the fence, sun-browned, naked children and wary, ragged adults, mothers with babies slung on their backs. Surely they too had not eaten in days.

Afraid, Arjani realized, or it felt like a realization to her fogged mind. All that delicious fruit, all those calories, and no one would eat them. It was magic blinding the others, keeping them away. Magic, the handiwork of the *hantu* .

She was not aware that her feet were carrying her past the gate until a firm hand fell on her shoulder, turned her round. Her father was looking down at her, shaking his head. "It's no good, *anak*," he said, his voice shuddering even though his eyes were bright and dry. "We can't eat their food. It will kill us."

"Special deal." The woman pleaded, her smile faltering at the prospect of losing a sale. "Uncle, it's a special deal today. Anything you can spare."

The seller's hair was patchy: it had fallen out in clumps, and raw, red sores flared on the exposed skin of her neck. This was important, but Arjani couldn't remember why. Her sluggish, sugar-starved brain spun in a pattern of confused impressions. The woman, the clustered refugees, the dusty road – the fragments spun away from her, tumbled into one another. Bapak caught her as she swayed and held her up.

"We all eat it." The farmer woman's voice was drifting in from across a great distance, from the other side of the ocean. "There's nothing wrong with it. We don't go hungry. Neither do our children."

Arjani became aware that her father was carrying her in his arms. Away from the starving crowd at the fence, who were creeping cautiously forward, hunger overriding their fear of the blight.

"We have to stay strong," he spoke into her ear. "There are too many of us in here. Not enough food. Things will get harder, but it's not the time to throw caution to the wind."

"Those people are from the villages," Arjani said. Something about that was important, but she had trouble remembering what it was. The feel of mango fibers between her teeth, sweet juice pouring down her throat: that was all she could focus on. A single mango couldn't hurt her. "*Bapak*, they have food. They want to share with us."

"They're mad," her father said. "It's the poisons from the blight. They can't think straight. That's what will happen to you if you eat the food they've grown. A long, painful death."

What will happen if we don't eat, then? Arjani wanted to ask but didn't. Hot dust swirled around her feet as Bapak set her down. Her knees wobbled, but she kept her balance. All the way into the barracks building, she could feel her father's presence behind her, waiting to catch her if she started to fall.

Moisture shimmering on emerald leaves. Long, musty shadows inside, quiet now, empty of people. Arjani made it to the raffia sleeping mat, laid down, and went away for a moment. Came back to the feel of her mother's hands pressing a cool compress against her forehead, the back of her neck. To the noise of her parents murmuring urgently. Then: sweetness on her lips, her whole body responding to it, coming to life.

Ibu's cache of food, secreted in a hole in the blackened wall. High-glucose tubers, worth more than their weight in gold. Gold that had once adorned Ibu's slender wrists and neck, wooden boxes full of jewelry locked in the family vault. A vault in a house lost under the waves. All the things they'd lost on their way here, to nothing.

Arjani lay suspended between worlds, listening to her mother's quiet sobs, Bapak's attempts at consoling his wife. Maybe this was all an illusion, a fever dream. Maybe they had never left the island. Maybe they were still in the house, dark water whispering over their heads. Their own *hantu*, haunting themselves, locked in a cycle of guilt and shame.

A corporation had bought the camp and was taking over its management. Like flotsam after a low tide, the remaining survivors of Tambak Eleven gathered in the central clearing to watch the new administrators move in, their black mechanical birds taking off and landing in a flurry of dust and frenetic activity.

Already the weathered, damp-rotted buildings had been removed, replaced by spotless white prefabs that fit into one another like jigsaw pieces. The fallen fencing was in the process of being torn out, tireless autolayers erecting a concrete wall around the perimeter. Billows of dust and construction printer debris sailed across the camp, depositing a pale, persistent layer on every available surface, forcing Bapak to repeatedly take off his glasses and clean them on the hem of his starched new shirt. The arrival of the *bules* had heralded changes that bordered on the miraculous: water supply fixed, latrines emptied, a big hospital popping up on the southern edge of the Tambak overnight, dispensing free medicine. It also had a thinking screen that could scan someone with invisible rays and diagnose them in under an hour. Most importantly, the food, which included rice cakes, fresh fruit and vegetables, krill and SoyPro patties, was readily available, tasty, abundant, and handed out by smiling employees. Real milk was flowing from great metal urns at the back of the new dining hall.

There were a few malcontents among the refugees, grumbling about the government ceding control of the *tambaks* to the Europeans. But these voices were growing fewer and further between. Shelter, security, full stomachs were concepts that had become alien during the long months of exile. The *bules* had revived faith in things getting better, and the residents of Tambak Eleven were ready to believe.

"Here they come," a villager said, standing next to Bapak in the crowd. "Our saviors."

A man dressed in white was approaching from the administrative building, a *bule* man with long legs, striding quickly across the heat-wilted grass. Another man trailed behind him, a local clad in the same uniform, but small and thin, a head shorter than the European. There was no doubt who was in charge.

The European paused in front of the refugees. Smiled broadly and addressed them in English, then in Dutch. Arjani could speak both languages, but her gut feeling told her not to give herself away. She glanced at Bapak, who shook his head quickly, without looking at her. He too must have sensed it was better not to stand out, better to blend into the crowd.

The second man translated loudly enough for everyone to hear. "We are here on behalf of the Company," he said, emphasizing the last word. "Glasser-Kamada has assumed responsibility for the administration of Tambak Eleven. It is part of our agreement with the government." He gestured at the gate, where a group of shirtless laborers were wrestling a holodeck in place, running cables across the ground. "Do not be alarmed," the interpreter said. "The camp is now corporate property. But you, the people, are not. You are free to leave with your families, if you wish to do so."

"He thinks we've never seen a hologram before," Komang whispered, and was immediately shushed.

"Where did the soldiers go?" a man shouted from the crowd. "What do you want from us?"

"Under our administration," the interpreter went on, even though the European had not said a word, "we hope to establish a prosperous and sustainable future for your new community. A place where every citizen-consumer will be in charge of their own pursuit of happiness. We hope to ensure your full cooperation in this endeavor."

The crowd shifted and muttered while they sweated under the sun. The European cleared his throat and spoke, his smile unwavering. "Glasser-Kamada is committed to global wellbeing," came the translation. "We wish to eradicate the diseases that have ravaged your community and your nation. Using cutting-edge technologies, we will end the blight on your crop fields. It is our duty as participants in the glorious global free market, as good partners to your government, to enable every man, woman, and child to live a better life. Reclaiming, rebuilding, providing education for all. A life free of disease and hunger and poverty, full of hope."

Arjani watched the European's sweaty face as the interpreter spoke. Flushed from the sun, thin hair plastered to his scalp, his face never lost its eager, pleasant expression. It was a familiar expression, the one she understood all *bules* put on for each other. False like a mask, but so ingrained in their way of life that it was considered the height of bad manners not to respond with a corresponding one of your own. When those masks slipped, the underlying ugliness would be exposed for a brief moment, red like raw meat, eyes suffused by a demonic glow from within, as if their soul was on fire. That's what Mbah Sastri had told her. It had to be uncomfortable, she thought, carrying all that heat inside one's skin, tormented by internal fires even as one slept.

Now she watched the European's eyes for traces of that infernal flame, but they were blank, untouched by his affable smile. He held out his hands with the palms out, as if to show he meant no harm. "We all have a part to play in building a better future," he said in Dutch. "Private capital has the potential to overcome political divisions and bureaucratic ineptitude. To eliminate malnutrition and stunted growth in children. To guarantee a dignified old age for seniors. In the days to come, our experts will offer free medscans to all residents of Tambak Eleven. Free treatment to all in need, at a level of service comparable to that of any corporate clinic. This is our pledge to you, with our name and reputation put up as collateral."

He ended his speech with a few phrases of gratitude in broken Bahasa, which brought out good-natured laughter from everyone in the crowd, even Mbah Sastri. The interpreter wrapped up by giving them the gist of the European's words, adding on a few verbal flourishes to signify respect. Evidently pleased with themselves, the men in white made their way back to the administration building. Hot and hungry, the crowd began to disperse.

Pak Lintang's face shone with sweat and eagerness. "You heard the *tuwan*," he repeated excitedly as the islanders filed back to their new bungalows, a replacement for the stuffy, musty dormitories. "Those are the words of progress. Of science. We are saved. A few months, and we'll all be on our feet again. Ready to leave this *tambak* and live like human beings again."

Bapak only waggled his head, neither agreeing nor disagreeing openly. Mbah had no such compunctions. "I won't let those *bule* devils anywhere near me," she announced to anyone within earshot. "The doctors at our town hospital – those were true healers. This one is not a doctor, but a public speaker. A storyteller. Did you see his hands? Eh!" She gestured for emphasis. "Those are not a doctor's hands. Those are not a doctor's eyes. Those are the hands and eyes of a bean counter. Don't tell me otherwise."

Wanting no part in the argument, Bapak muttered, hid his face behind a months-old newspaper, yellow pages and ink smudged by his obsessive reading and rereading. Arjani was sure that her father could, if pressed, quote entire articles from memory, from this edition, or from any of the ones in the treasured bundle under his cot. But this time his gaze seemed to stray from the page, like he was chewing on the administrator's remark, finding it indigestible.

"They want to help," Ibu said with deference, unwilling to openly contradict her mother-in-law. "Yet they ask for nothing. Why would they do it?"

Grandmother frowned at her. "Why do the *bule* do anything, daughter? Because they are possessed, that's why. They can't control themselves. Besides, the whole world has gone crazy, and the *bule* were crazy to begin with. We should pray that their madness doesn't bring down some even worse misfortune upon us."

Arjani's surfacing from the dream was so light, so gradual, that she barely noticed it until the shape of the room assembled around her. An unfamiliar place, empty, terrifying, its walls so white they almost glowed in the dark.

For a moment she was disoriented, then she remembered where she was. Moving into the family bungalow, the smell of new plaster and composites fresh from the construction printer, tiny particles lingering in the air. It wasn't unfamiliar, and it wasn't empty either. Faint snoring filled the darkness: her family were around her, still, shapeless lumps on their cots. The European *tuwan* had claimed his company was here to help, but she wasn't ready to believe him. She would find out for herself in person.

Slowly, Arjani lowered her bare feet onto the resin floor. Waited with bated breath to make sure no one had woken up. As silent as the *hantu*, she crossed to the door, opened it, and stepped out.

Soft lamps illuminated the camp's perimeter, glowed over the entrances to the buildings. Beyond the light, the vast blackness of night spread its wings, the deep shadows of the trees towering over the walls. Not a soul was about, but Arjani wasn't fooled. Invisible eyes were watching her every move, swiveling to track her as she made her way along the neat rows of white structures, toward the center of Tambak Eleven.

Lights everywhere, driving back the shadows, exposing every square meter of the camp enclosure. No secrets could be kept in such persistent illumination, no conditions achieved for a meaningful haunting: even the *hantu* shunned this unnatural glow, retreated deeper into the forest, where the day never penetrated.

Disappointed, Arjani rounded a construction site and was heading back to her bungalow when a section of the lights went out, plunging one corner of the camp into complete darkness.

Arjani froze in her tracks, expecting some sort of alarm to go off. Was it her doing? An entire section of the wall had been swallowed by darkness, leaving pale afterimages floating in her vision. She waited to see if any of the guards were alerted, then raced toward the section of the wall, her heart beating fast.

Faint light shimmered between the black trees, suddenly visible in contrast. A pale blue radiance, moving among the branches. In the brief interval between the camp beacons going out and the surging tide of darkness, Arjani saw two shapes appear in the canopies. She flinched from them, swallowing a cry more of surprise than of terror.

A man and a woman were standing on a high branch, looking directly at her. Leaves and branches intruding through their transparent, luminous outlines. Gone before she could be sure she'd seen anything.

Ghosts. Arjani's mind spun with the impossibility of it for a dizzy moment. Then she had to clap a hand over her mouth to suppress her laughter. It had been a hologram, like the corporate logo above the gate. Like the alien monsters and spacefarers at the TransCore Future Horizons park Bapak had taken her to when she was little. So these were the *hantu* from Mbah Sastri's stories. But where did the hologram come from?

She moved quietly along the wall, listening to the somnolent night breath of the forest. No one was there, at least no one she could hear. Which made sense: ghost feet did not make noise. But she thought she heard a low whirring, a sound that wasn't quite a sound, like the flutter of dragonfly wings.

There. The holograms were now inside the camp, less than fifty meters from where she was standing. Arms extended, pointing at her, then toward the administration complex. As if inviting her to look.

Breathless, Arjani raced in the direction the blue silhouettes indicated, taking care to keep to the dark and out of sight. Behind her, the lights were snapping back on, entire swathes of the camp materializing from thin air, night watchmen striding between the buildings. She managed to crouch behind a power transformer before their flashlights swept across her. This is what the ghosts were trying to show her. The low, long building of the clinic, now shuttered and silent, save for a lonely guard dozing in a chair by the entrance.

She shrank deeper into the shadows as a ripple passed through the perimeter lights, dimming and turning them back on, causing confusion among the stunned guards. When their heavy footsteps trod past her hiding place, she ran back to the bungalows, confused herself, until she found the right number.

The door yielded to her fingers. Someone coughed in the sleeping area but didn't wake up. Arjani slipped under her covers, tried to calm her breathing. There was no doubt about it. Whoever had put on the hologram show outside had done so for her benefit. Yet no matter how hard she racked her brain, she could not come up with a reason why.

It wasn't until she was already drifting off to sleep that the blinking lights flashed through her mind's eye. Not a malfunction, or random sabotage, but a repeating pattern. Long flashes interspersed with short ones, spelling out a message. A message that followed her past the veil of sleep, filling her with cold dread.

GET OUT

The Company seemed determined to stay true to its word.

Within the first week of new ownership, the residents of Tambak Eleven had all been scanned, categorized, triaged where necessary. Within two weeks, techs in self-contained biohazard suits had trekked down into the exclusion zone and treated those they could for viruses and parasites before bringing them back. By the end of the month, the population of Tambak Eleven doubled. Miraculously, there was still food for everyone.

"Genetically enhanced," Bapak said, clicking his chopsticks over his bowl of *goreng*. "Top quality. When the government bigwigs sit down to eat dinner tonight, they will be served this very same rice."

He sounded happy, Arjani thought, like himself for the first time since the evacuation. His gaunt face had filled in somewhat, and he had cultivated a small paunch, which he was embarrassingly proud of. "Eat up," he said, nudging Arjani and motioning at her eldest daughter. "It is good."

By week five, every camp resident was issued a fresh set of uniforms. Three colors: yellow, blue, and white. Ibu, Bapak and Komang were all yellow, while Arjani and Mbah Sastri received white garments. Samita wore blue, which she was very pleased with. Nothing to worry about, the new administrator said, just a measure to better meet the health needs of the residents, watch for trends.

There was a new administrator almost every week, all Europeans of indeterminate age, all well-groomed and smiling, all almost aggressively polite. From morning until dusk, Tambak Eleven was a mayhem of humming construction printers and clamoring machinery. New wings were being added to the clinic, all plasteel and carbon-fiber polymers, the resulting structure looking like a honeycomb of tightly interconnected hexagonal units. "More rooms," the new administrator explained, or her predecessor had. "We need additional beds as we keep expanding. Your government is very pleased by our collaborative effort."

At night, Arjani lay awake for hours, waiting for the noise outside to subside so she could sneak out again. But now there were always people moving through the camp, vehicles or workers or patrolling watchmen. Some of the guards had started carrying guns and would chase indoors any residents caught outside their bungalow after dark.

"It's for everyone's protection," was the official line from camp management. "Many of our residents have serious health conditions that require monitoring. This way we always know where to find you."

This was met with lukewarm protest, which quickly tapered out to mere grumbling. Even Bapak, initially suspicious of the *bule* takeover, seemed appeased. A man of order and logic, he had regained his appreciation for regular meals and running water.

"We need to be safe," he would say, pushing his brand-new, Company-provided spectacles up the bridge of his thin nose. "Too many good-for-nothings in this camp, complaining and idling about. You never know what people like that will get up to."

The monsoons abated, the smell of damp loam and vegetation overlaying the construction dust, thick mists rolling in from the trees. Arjani went about her business under a cloud of tense anticipation. *Get out.* Surely the spirits were angry and would wreak vengeance upon the Tambak any minute now. Fire and lightning and destruction, like in the old legends. But the days went by, and the camp remained standing. No supernatural retribution descended from the skies and no bandit army emerged from the jungle to storm the gates. The machines churned on, excavators and cranes bending the earth to their will.

"This is how we work together," the new administrator told the few residents who still bothered to attend the public gatherings. "This is how we build a sustainable tomorrow."

Once a week, every resident was summoned to the clinic. Blues first, then yellows, the whites going last. Some of them underwent a battery of incomprehensible tests, others received transdermal patches or injections, others were simply asked to stand in the medscanner for a few minutes. Arjani went twice, and both times was shown a sequence of stained cardboard pieces, to which she had to respond with one-word descriptions. Each time she was asked to trade in her uniform for a new one. Another week, and the colors would be summoned in reverse order, based on some convoluted and mysterious logic. Bapak would become agitated before each visit: after, he sat inside the bungalow and stared at nothing, refusing to speak for hours, doubt carving lines in his once-youthful face.

The family was moved to a different section of the camp, away from the other islanders. "Like we're pieces in a *dam-da-man* game," Ibu said once after dinner. "Not living people." Immediately she seemed contrite, glancing from side to side as if afraid of being overheard.

Arjani kept her mouth shut and counted. There was a meaning to the changing uniform colors, a pattern to be discerned, like the ghosts' Morse code. The key to unlocking it evaded her, but the message was an important one. An uneasy voice at the back of her mind told her that she didn't have much time left to solve it.

New faces appeared in Tambak Eleven; old ones disappeared just as abruptly. "Resettlement programs," came the cheerful announcement. "Get you back on your feet in no time." Animated posters went up around the communal areas, showing clean, smiling families posed in front of residential complexes. Bapak grumbled but signed the family up. "We can't let the past drown us," he said to Ibu, in a rare argument. "Our old life will not return. But we can build a new one, with the help of the Europeans."

Soon Arjani lost track of the color changes and of medicines shot under or stuck onto her skin, or inhaled, or swallowed on a sugar cube. A better future would make it all worth it, erase the worry from her parents' faces, bring the light back into Mbah Sastri's eyes. But deep down she felt the cold, clammy breath of the *hantu* settling over her hopes like a fog, ghostly hands clutching at her, pulling her back.

Arjani's color for the week was blue, and so was her little brother's. Ibu was the only family member who received a yellow uniform. She held it up with a weak smile, but Arjani could tell her mother was shaken.

"What does it mean?" Mbah asked, looking concerned.

"Nothing," Bapak said, with a dismissive gesture. "It's just the doctors' way of keeping track." But he took Ibu's hand when he didn't think anyone was looking, held it just a second too long. Both of them looked terrified and lost, like children themselves.

When the signal sounded over the speakers, Arjani walked out of the bungalow and joined the column of blue-clad residents heading for the clinic. Her hand gripped Komang's a bit too tightly, until he squirmed and whined at her to let him go. "I'm not a baby," he said, pointedly stepping away from her. "I won't get lost on the way there, you know."

Arjani was only half-listening. There was a commotion at one of the new construction sites, the lines of people breaking up into clusters, gawking over the barriers. A handful of guards tried to restore order but did little to add to the general noise. Dragging Komang behind her, Arjani pushed as close as she could to the front, crouched to peek through the fencing.

The machines had gone insane. Several of them whirled in place, or traced the same senseless routes over and over, smashing into each other. An excavator had run over a row of barriers and flipped on its side, its treads turning over in the air, lights blinking on and off. Frightened workers huddled behind a pile of blocks, staring at the mechanical frenzy.

"*Hantu*," someone said behind her. "That's their doing."

Arjani turned round to look at her brother. Komang's face was set and serious, his gaze blundering past her, at the machines. "I see them too," he said. "They come at night. Sometimes a man, sometimes a woman, and sometimes both."

"When did you see them?"

Her brother shrugged, kicked at a clump of dirt. Arjani fought down a surge of irritation: he was just a child, he could not understand any of it. "What did they tell you?" she said.

Haunted eyes looked up at her. "They showed me things," he said as they rejoined the clinic-goers. "They showed me what's in the new hospital. The things they do there."

"What is that?"

Komang seemed about to speak, then changed his mind, his lips squeezed tightly shut. Pulling his hand out of her grasp, he ran off to join a group of blue-clad boys yelling and playing in front of the clinic.

Dazed by his words, Arjani followed the line as if in a dream. The ghosts were restless, reaching over the wall to touch the living. She couldn't tell what this meant, but something about it made her nervous. The blunt warning, the machines malfunctioning: it all seemed to point to an approaching crisis, some inauspicious turn of events.

Ibu returned from her test and lay down on her cot right away. "Just a touch of the heat," she said, straining to sound reassuring. Mbah Sastri waved the children outside, dimmed the lights. "Your mother will feel better without your noise," she said, closing the door. "Let her sleep and recover."

But evening came, and Ibu was still abed. Distraught, Bapak raced over to the clinic, came back with the duty doctor, who checked Ibu's pulse and made a great production of waving around a handheld scanner. After a few minutes of going through the motions, the doctor stepped outside to consult with the specialist team. Arjani couldn't make out the whispers, but the alarm in the doctor's posture was evident.

"Your wife is healthy," the doctor said to Bapak when she came back in, offering a bland, professional smile. She spoke the language well, but with a pronounced accent and without nuances. "This is just a reaction to something she was given last week. Unpleasant at times, but not dangerous."

"Can you help her?" Bapak said, biting his lip.

"I'll take her to the clinic myself." The doctor helped Ibu off the cot, turned the beam of her smile at Arjani and her siblings. "We'll have her back in no time at all."

Arjani wanted to cry, to lash out. Instead, she tamped down her anger and smiled back at the doctor. Out of the corner of her eye, she sensed movement just past the open door. A gleam of pale blue light against the falling dusk. No one else seemed to notice it, let alone react to it.

Was it the real *hantu*?

Cold seeped around her shoulders, or perhaps it was just her overwrought nerves. There was no time to consider other possibilities. With the guards distracted by the chaos at the construction site and the spirits nearby, she had to act, and quickly. "We can all go to the clinic," she said, feeling a giddy mix of terror and exhilaration. "Ibu will feel better if she knows we're there with her."

The doctor turned to Bapak with a let's-be-reasonable expression. "I can't let you all in. Protocol won't allow it."

"Please, Madam." Bapak seemed confused by Arjani's request, but he went along with it. He put on his best face that he presented to the *bule* – the shuffling, superstitious villager trying to ingratiate himself. "Only to the clinic entrance and back. The children are upset. It will mean so much to them."

Arjani's breath stopped in her throat as the doctor contemplated this new twist. It seemed like a small concession, whatever got this people moving and out of her way. Even Mbah Sastri, sensing a shift in the atmosphere, waved at Komang to help her off her cot. "Okay," the doctor finally said. "Only to the entrance."

The family trudged out of the bungalow, Arjani and Bapak speaking loudly, waving their arms in the air. Ibu frowned and rubbed at her temples. The doctor seemed exasperated. "Wait for me," she said sharply, her mask of politeness slipping. "Is this everyone?"

Above the door, the lamp flickered, flared. Arjani squeezed her eyes at the light, counting the pulses. She felt the rough ground under her thin shoes as she pivoted onto the balls of her feet, shifting her slight weight, the muscles in her legs tensing with anticipated effort. Her timing had to be just right.

"Please, Madam Doctor," she said, gesturing wildly, pointing behind the doctor's back, into the bungalow. "You're forgetting Ibu. She needs to come with us."

Confusion wrinkled the doctor's smooth forehead. Her lips formed a moue of surprise as she saw the figure in yellow, sitting on Ibu's cot.

"But I just—" The doctor's foot hovered over the threshold as she leaned forward, peering into the bungalow, off balance. "Your mother is right outside. I—"

Arjani moved closer, shifting her center of gravity lower. Laid a gentle hand on the doctor's low back. Light and silent, like the touch of a ghost. "Look closer," she said, and when the doctor obeyed, she threw all her weight behind her arm and hip. Like a *silat* wrestler, or a warrior slashing an opponent with her sword.

With a strangled *oomph* of surprise, the doctor pitched forward, through the doorway, and fell sprawling to the floor. Arjani slammed the door shut, head spinning from the rush of adrenaline. Heard the bolts click as an invisible hand guided them home.

Mbah Sastri's eyes were wide with surprise. From inside the bungalow came muffled shouts, the noise of fists hammering on the door. "Why did you do that?" Bapak said to Arjani, a horrified expression stretching his features downward.

"No time to explain," Arjani said. "We must be quick." Her eyes roamed the forest outside the *tambak*, desperate for a sign. There. Just above the top of the wall, four houses down, a bright yellow orb danced in the leaves, casting no light. *Another ghost.* As soon as Arjani approached, the light skipped further down the wall.

It wanted to show her a way out, she realized. But how would her loved ones get over the wall? Her grandmother could not climb it, and neither could Ibu, especially in her current state.

From the gate came voices raised in alarm, flashlight beams slashing through the dusk. Arjani sought the light again. "Over there," she said, dragging Komang by the arm. "Hurry. Follow the light."

When she turned around, she realized they were no longer following her. Bapak stood as if rooted to the ground, looking helpless, Ibu leaning on his arm, his older daughter on his other side, face flushed with tears. Mbah Sastri had also halted, wheezing from the exertion.

"We are safe here," Bapak said, reciting like a schoolboy. "The Company takes care of us. Your mother needs the doctors at the clinic."

"It's not a clinic, *bapak*." Arjani glanced past his shoulder. Running figures were halfway on their sprint from the gate, more lights joining them. "These people don't want to help us. Come on. We can't stay."

"We have nowhere to go."

"They're making us sick," Arjani said. "That's what they did to *ibu*. That's what they'll do to everyone who stays."

Emotions mixed on her father's face. He raced to the section of the wall that the orb had paused over. Tapped the panels until one rang hollow. Took a step back and kicked it hard, smashing a hole in the thin partition. Again and again, until he'd made a wide enough gap.

"We can't go," he said, placing one hand on her shoulder, the other on her brother's. Smiling through his tears. "We are old, and slow. They will catch us. But you two can run. You can find a place far away from here. Forget about us." *We're already memories*, his eyes told her. *Already* hantu.

Arjani wanted to scream at him, to break down and cry. Instead, she roused herself to action, scrambling through the hole, Komang following on her heels. As soon as she was on the other side, she glanced back through the opening.

Bapak was walking toward the approaching guards, arms outstretched. For the first time in months, in years, he looked the way Arjani remembered him: upright and proud, a small, physically unassuming man, yet looming like a giant in the floodlights.

Then she was running, crashing through the wet foliage, following Komang's vanishing silhouette into the jungle, the orb of light floating ahead of them, guiding them out of the shadowland.

They half-waded, half-swam through the flooded fields. "Over here," a voice called out to them from the darkness of the mangrove swamp. A boat was bobbing on the still surface of the water under the causeway. The voice was unfamiliar, but Arjani and Komang didn't hesitate for a moment.

Eager hands pulled them in, gave them dry clothes and blankets. Three adults and a young girl sat inside, shifted round to make room for the arrivals. The boat was one of the old models with a repurposed alcohol engine, filled with shaded faces and low, urgent voices. Its single light was turned off as they puttered into the night, coasting along the mangrove banks in silence.

Unseen birds screeched over the water, the black sky speckled with thousands of stars, like scattered diamonds. Arjani closed her eyes, feeling the motion of the river under the weathered floorboards. Curled an arm around Komang, the quiet sobs racking his body transferring through the muscle and bone, keeping beat with her own.

When the trees thickened and the current became stronger, the boaters turned their lights back on, gave the two children hot tea and snacks.

"We didn't think anyone had seen our signals," said a thin, kind-looking woman with large dark eyes. "Every night we came and broadcast our message. But it's been weeks since anyone responded."

"We were almost caught by their security patrols." A man grinned at the helm, startling white teeth in a face the color of teakwood. "The soldiers didn't give us much trouble, but this corporation is a whole different story. The second time we hacked in, they were waiting for us. That was a close call too."

"Are more coming?" This came from a European man, his hair and beard near all silver, his face deeply lined.

Arjani shook her head. "Just us," she said. "We're the only ones who made it out."

The kind-faced woman looked dejected, prompting the European to pat her forearm. "We'll come back," the woman said. "We always come back. There have to be at least a few more people we can smuggle out."

"We have a deal with the smugglers," White Teeth explained to Arjani. "Their services don't come cheap. But no cost is too high, even if we can only save a few. We've seen the pharma camps before, and the horror they leave behind."

Arjani said nothing. She stared ahead at the moonlit surface of the river, the dark cutouts of the trees.

"You'll be okay," White Teeth said. Filled her cup from a thermos. "It's hard at first. But it beats staying in the camp."

A familiar whirring noise cut through the air above the boat. Arjani flinched, instinctively shielding Komang with her body. Then she saw the girl in the back of the boat, a slip of a girl, really, not much older than herself. She sat so perfectly still as to be unnoticeable, wrapped in a hooded sweatshirt several sizes too large.

A slim hand gestured and two drones descended over the boat, touched down at the girl's bare feet. She sighed, removing her lenses. Caught Arjani's glance, gave her a wry smile. "Camera drones," she said. "I added some console 'ware, cross-stitched with an old home entertainment system. But it still works. You don't get this resolution quality with the new viewcasts."

Another wave of her hand, and light burst from the drones, resolved into the apparitions Arjani had seen back in the camp. The man and the woman floated over her, gesturing, pointing. Pale forms through which the girl's grinning face intruded, her lips forming a voiceless word. *Magic.*

"Like ghosts," Arjani said. Reached one hand out to caress a drone's plastic wing, damp with condensation.

The girl laughed, switched off the projection. "If you believe in ghosts," she said softly, "you might just happen to meet a few."

Hugging her knees to her chest, Arjani sat in the boat, free and untethered, and let the slow-moving current carry her onward.

CARRIERS

The quarantine guards held up the train at every checkpoint, marching up and down the aisles, rummaging through the compartments and the baggage, checking and rechecking stamped passes and ident cards. They complained of malfunctioning scanners, of bureaucratic chaos causing delays in proper authorizations – difficulties that could be instantly resolved by a bribe. Myung-soo's cameras and lenses were a constant draw. *Newscan star*, they would say, rubbing thumbs and forefingers together, the universal sign for money. *It must pay well to be getting all those hits and views. How about a cup of hot tea for a couple of overworked uncles?*

Myung-soo kept his reactions in check and played the ignorant yuppie. He grinned until his facial muscles ached, pointed his viewfinder at the greedy guards until they scowled and scuttled away. The world, Myung-soo had learned early on, belonged to idiots, put idiots in charge and kept them there, rewarded idiocy: therefore it made sense for one to act like an idiot, or as close to an idiot as one could, in order to survive. He paid bribes when he could not avoid them, but got out of the conurb mostly unmolested, his equipment intact, the bottle of *soju* stashed in his duffel bag unopened until the last of the sprawling outskirts fell behind the train. Then he popped the cork, poured two fingers of the clear liquor into a plastic cup, and toasted his good luck in the glow of the compartment's biolumes.

It had taken him months of string-pulling and a small fortune in facilitation fees to finagle a seat on this trip. If Lady Luck continued to smile upon him – and Myung-soo had a streak kilometers long, better than any gambler – the Big Media Companies would descend on his feed like vultures, fighting tooth and nail over his photos, showering him in royalties.

In his line of work, money came and went at the behest of the capricious pageview gods: feast when he hit on a scoop, famine when he didn't, which was most of the time. Every feed and every channel carried images of piles of dead from virus and starvation, or of mass protests against the fourth caretaker government in as many years, or of ragged mobs fighting over UN food shipments from the orbital colonies. Myung-soo had been patient. He had invested what little influence he had strategically, and now he had his big exclusive story. A seat on the supply train to the Red Zone, accompanied by medical and relief workers and the inevitable handful of low-caliber politicos jostling for media opportunities.

The train passed makeshift shantytowns, tin-roofed plastifoam shacks, kilometers of barbed wire – enclaves where the refugees had tried to hide from the superflu, to isolate themselves from the dying villages, then the dying suburbs. With an incubation period of mere hours, and a survival rate of less than twenty per cent, the virus finally seemed to have burned itself out, killing off enough millions to guarantee its own extinction. The last of the known infected had been penned into the Red Zone, a pre-Unification military base repurposed into the nation's largest viral containment camp. There they awaited recovery, or death, or the increasingly elusive cure, well-provisioned and isolated, guarded by soldiers and cared for by teams of medics. Despite all of Myung-soo's research and generosity in the Itaewon bars, no source, government or otherwise, could confirm the number of detainees, or which units were still at their posts, or the names of pharma transnationals operating inside the Red Zone. No photojournalist had ever set foot within its gates. It was pristine source material, and Myung-soo was determined to carve it out for his own. He hoped to capitalize on the sacrifice made by the first responders, an overlooked side to the superflu, not as spectacular as the death and horror and stacked bodies rotting under plastic sheets. A simple but powerful human interest tale of selflessness and the belief in a greater cause. If Myung-soo could break that story, his fortune and fame would be made.

It was slow going. Even here, far from the checkpoints or any signs of human habitation, the train still braked to a crawl along the more dilapidated sections of the track. The railways had all but collapsed in the absence of government subsidies, and the invisible hand of the market had yet to apply its benevolent touch to these blighted parts. Abandoned villages, emptied by disease and poverty alike, cut off from utility supply chains, lay along the line like plastic blocks scattered by a petulant child.

Myung-soo dozed, and read, and dozed some more, refreshing himself with overpriced beer and snacks from the improvised cafe car. Most of the compartments had been converted to cargo holds, with the passengers scattered throughout the front part of the train, heeding some incomprehensible hierarchy – the politicos in first class, the scientists and techs in standard, nervous and haunted-looking. Myung-soo was relegated to the very last car to emphasize his lowly status among the elites. It didn't bother him. He knew that soon enough they'd be lining up for him to take their photo, dropping his name at Party conventions and soirees, fawning over him.

Black birds were fluttering over the barbed wire, landing on it with ungainly grace, and darting down to pick at the body hanging in the razored coils.

Myung-soo swallowed hard, sweat breaking out under his arms and the small of his back. But his eyes and hands knew what they were doing, even as his stomach turned from the sight: they were running on muscle memory, reaching for his camera, lining up frames and angles, snapping pictures through the smudged train window. He was in his element now, shooting and shifting and shooting again, part of him horrified, another part observing with the cold detachment of the professional.

The figure tangled in the wire seemed to float in the air, a gory and decayed saint casting a benediction at the slowing train. A man, judging by the height and set of the shoulders, dressed in what looked like a lab coat and scrub pants. Bare feet dangling without touching the ground, his face obscured by longish, blood-matted hair, his arms stretched out wide. Dark rust streaked the corpse's white garments in places where sharp beaks had not already shredded them to ribbons, trying to get at the dead flesh underneath. It wasn't possible to tell what the man had died of, or whether he had died on the fence, or simply been hung on it like a grisly ornament.

Myung-soo frowned behind his viewfinder, used his powerful lens to zoom in as close as he could. In all the footage he'd seen of the camp, the doctors and nurses and techs had worn biohazard suits, not lab coats. Was the body on the fence a sign of safety protocols breaking down past the point of no return? Whatever the reason, this was pure gold, an even bigger story than he had anticipated. He tried to take another shot, but the body was now too far, black clouds of birds obscuring it. The train was slowing down, pulling into the station, the moving platform coming to a stop outside the car windows.

He jerked back from the window, thoughts suddenly blank, as his brain recoiled from the nightmare on the other side of the glass.

It wasn't just one body. There were dozens of them, perhaps a hundred slung up on the barbed-wire fence right behind the platform. Some were naked, some clothed, all bloody and stiff. Flocks of crows hopped around them, poking at them halfheartedly, like bloated diners at the end of a holiday meal.

A mass breakout attempt, Myung-soo told himself. That's what it had to be. Somehow the infected had overwhelmed their guards, made it all the way to the outer perimeter before being stopped by the wire. The bodies were all suspended in the same pose, feet hovering, arms flung out, as if they'd tried to take synchronized flight before being impaled.

Outside, the platform stood dark and empty. The only thing moving were the crows.

He waited for the recorded voice making the safety arrangements to chime from the speakers, but his compartment remained silent. Pressing his face to the window, he strained to see what was happening further to the left and right of his car. There: a group of figures was entering through one of the

First Class doors. They looked armed and uniformed. Myung-soo breathed a little easier. Someone was still in charge here; someone would explain what was happening.

His fragile hope was shattered by the noise of gunshots ringing out through the carriage.

Frozen by indecision and terror, Myung-soo stood by the window. He prayed for the train to start rolling again, away from the awful platform, away from the rotting death grinning at him from the fence. But the journey was over: he was at the end of the line.

He was still motionless, camera half-raised in his trembling hands, when the door to his car hissed open and two men walked in.

Mechanically, Myung-soo reached for his hazmat kit, remembering the safety drill the Ministry had made him go through before departure. The men watched him from the door as he pulled on his filter mask. They were dirty, dressed in hand-me-down clothes, faces grimy but determined. Both were armed, but their submachineguns were slung around their necks.

"You don't need that," the older man said, pointing to Myung-soo's mask.

The photographer's throat constricted as he realized that neither intruder was wearing protective gear, that they had just come in from the camp, that infected air was, in all likelihood, wafting into the compartment, all around him. "The virus," he said, waving his hands, lost for words. Did they not understand the danger?

"There is no virus here," said the other man. He plucked the mask from Myung-soo's shaking hands, tossed it onto the floor. His eyes were tired and hollow, but he was smiling. "Only good, clean country air."

"See for yourself," the older man said, stepping outside to motion Myung-soo to pass.

As if in a trance, Myung-soo obliged. The platform reeked of smoke and rotting flesh. He gagged and made to walk back into the train, the only safety his confused brain knew now. But the younger of the intruders was blocking his way, and the muzzle of the submachinegun was now level with his midsection.

The two armed men steered him down a set of stairs, into a drab cement building attached to the station. Its bare walls were scrawled with spray-painted slogans — A NEW AWAKENING was spelled out on one of them, another read END TOTALITARIAN CONTROL.

Myung-soo saw other armed figures dragging the remaining passengers out of the train, some of them wounded, some bloodied and unmoving. They were lined up at the edge of the platform and forced to their knees with weapons pointed at the backs of their heads. Mercifully, he was already out of sight when the first salvo rang out, the shots reverberating down the concrete corridors.

Even now, abducted at gunpoint by homicidal terrorists, unprotected against a deadly infection, Myung-soo's first instinct was to grab his camera and shoot.

No one stopped him and his captors as they entered the camp. No one was manning the sanitation checkpoints, or the broken, dusty medscanners. A solitary figure in army fatigues, a young woman, snapped to attention as they entered the circle of barracks.

"At ease," said the older man accompanying Myung-soo. He listened to the chatter coming through his earhook. "Looks like they're all accounted for," he said to his comrade.

"Welcome," the young woman said to Myung-soo. She smiled, and he took an involuntary step back, seeing the traces the disease had left on her – the crusted blood around the nose, the burst capillaries on her cheeks, the feverish glow in her eyes. But she shook her head gently, raised her hands in a placating gesture. "You shouldn't be afraid. There is no danger for you in this place. There never was."

As if a punchline to a morbid joke, a deep cough rattled from the center of her, doubling her over. The younger of his captors pushed Myung-soo forward. "It will be explained to you in a bit," he said.

"That girl was sick," Myung-soo said, trying to keep his voice calm and conversational. A surreal feeling took hold of him, like being inside a dream in which everyday, familiar things had been rearranged into nonsense. "She needs help. A doctor."

"She's fine." The older man's tone implied that he didn't wish to pursue the conversation further. When Myung-soo turned to look at the bodies hanging off the barbed wire, the muzzle of a submachinegun prodded him between the shoulderblades. "It's normal that you have questions. You have been fed lies for a long time. But have faith. Your eyes will be opened soon."

They marched him across the camp, to a warehouse building with an armed sentry posted in front. The inner circle, where Myung-soo's briefing materials had indicated the patient wards to be located, was mostly razed, the fencing torn down, the checkpoint prefabs burned down and vandalized. A single brick wall with a mural painted on it had been left standing. The mural depicted a gigantic man with fire blazing from his eyes and mouth. He was marching toward the viewer while figures of authority fled before him in exaggerated terror: a doctor, a soldier, a shifty-eyed man in a suit, presumably a government official. LET THE LIGHT PREVAIL was stenciled above the painting.

Without a word, the sentry raised the warehouse door and Myung-soo was hustled through into darkness.

Adjusted to daylight, his eyes could not make out more than dim outlines at first. But he sensed that he was not alone. The darkness stank of sweat, urine, and fear, a miasmic cloud. There others in the featureless room.

"Hello?" he said into the emptiness, carefully navigating around what smelled like a nightsoil bucket. "Hello? Can someone tell me what's going on?"

"Did the train come?" a voice spoke, startling him. Myung-soo could just about see the speaker, a short, stout man crouching further down the wall.

"Yes," Myung-soo said, keeping his distance. He couldn't tell where this was going, but maybe there was a story to be wrung out of the situation. "The train came. It's in the station."

"They walked right into the trap." This came from a woman, hoarse with illness, or disappointment. "We hoped the corpses would warn them something was wrong."

"What happened here?" Myung-soo's said. *Terrorism*, he thought dimly. *Terrorism, or some kind of catastrophic system failure.* "Where are the doctors? The authorities?"

"*We* are the authorities," the bald man said. "The doctors are all dead."

"What do you mean?"

But no answer came. Leaning back against the wall, Myung-soo clasped his arms around his tucked knees and tried not to think about anything. It was a mistake. It had to be. Someone would come along and explain everything eventually. To calm himself down, he visualized the finished piece in his head. A wide-angle shot of the camp to begin with, with the fire-breathing mural at the center. Then close-ups of the guards, the empty, bloody train station platform. It had the potential to become a syndicated feature, segueing to be bestseller.

He was distantly aware of the doors opening and closing, of a voice calling out names, of sobbing and coughing in the vagueness around him. When he heard his name being called, he rose on unsteady legs and tottered outside.

To his surprise, the last dregs of the day still hung in the sky, a livid redness in the west. Lights had come on along the camp perimeter, but only a few were working, the gaps between them getting longer the further one went from the barracks. More armed guards milled about, some in army or corporate security uniforms, others in a mishmash of civilian garments. Several had rifles, but others carried handguns and improvised weapons – knives, hammers, wrenches, even crude-looking spears made of blades tied to long poles.

Myung-soo was prodded into a long line of prisoners, all of whom looked just as confused and afraid as he felt. Suddenly it was hard to concentrate on the story. His mind went back to the kneeling figures on the platform, the executioners raising their guns, and his bladder felt loose, his knees weak.

A small detachment of guards escorted the procession to a low, long building decorated with the same incomprehensible slogans Myung-soo had seen before. Inside was a sort of dining area with plastic tables and long benches. Here each captive – Myung-soo could not think of a more appropriate term to describe himself and the others – was given a bowl of noodles and some bottled water. Without looking at one another, they sat down and began slurping, too terrified to speak.

Myung-soo allowed himself to relax a little. They were being fed. It didn't make sense to waste food on people you were planning to murder, especially since it looked like there was barely enough of it to go round. He bent his head over the bowl and shoveled the broth as fast as he could.

A shadow fell over him. Still chewing, Myung-soo looked up. Above him stood a soldierly type in a filthy uniform, asking for his name.

"Come with me," the guard said. He didn't sound threatening, or even particularly stern, and his pistol was holstered. "You're supposed to be a photographer. Do you have all your equipment with you?"

Dumbstruck, Myung-soo could only dip his head again, bobbing the camera slung around his neck. A sudden suspicion came to him that he was being tricked, set up for something terrible. If that was the case, it was too late. The guard had already started walking away, motioning Myung-soo to follow.

They went outside, crossed the fallen fences of the inner perimeter, to a round, domed structure. The guard opened a padlocked gate, ushered his charge up a long flight of stairs, then through a door, saluted, and left. A tired-looking middle aged woman raised her head from a dataconsole and stared at Myung-soo.

"Sit," she said, indicating a chair.

Myung-soo hurried to obey. The wall behind the woman was really a bank of tall windows overlooking what looked like a school gymnasium. People were moving down there, converging on a stage in the center of the shiny, brightly lit floor.

"Orientation ceremony," the woman said, nodding at the goings-on below. "For our new arrivals. We find it helpful to explain a few basic facts in a group setting. It makes people more receptive."

She coughed discreetly into the crook of her elbow, rattled her console keyboard, reading off Myung-soo's name, address, and personal information. "You were not on the original manifest," she said. "A rare bit of luck, then, that you're here. Your skills will be indispensable."

"Indispensable for what?" Myung-soo said, his voice very small. They wanted him to cooperate – another good sign. This woman was in a position of authority: if he did what she wanted him to do, he might still get his scoop.

"Getting the truth out to the world." The woman's face was solemn. "It's about time we did that. We have all been lied to for years. People have the right to know what really happened here."

"I'm afraid I don't understand." But Myung-soo *did* understand, for the first time since he'd come to the camp. This was familiar ground for him. Deep down, everyone wanted to tell their story. Maybe he'd get a quote or two to go with the pictures, squeeze a little bit of extra cash. Her eyes narrowed, as if she were trying to pry behind Myung-soo's face, to read his thoughts directly. "What do you know about this place? Or rather, what do you think you know?"

Myung-soo took a deep breath, silently counting to ten. He had the feeling that his next words would have to be chosen carefully. "Well," he drew out, "I heard that this is a treatment facility," he almost said *camp*, but caught himself, "for people infected with the superflu virus. That the government was re-searching a cure. Some kind of vaccine against it."

A grave nod of the head. "That was in my briefing before I was assigned here. But it wasn't true."

"It wasn't?"

"They lied." There was a moment of uncertainty in the official's eyes, immediately replaced by a flash of mindless rage. There and gone instantly as she brought it under control. "Yes, there was a virus. Yes, it was a flu, slightly more lethal than usual. But this camp wasn't set up to isolate the sick, or to research a cure. It was a social experiment."

She leaned back with a self-satisfied smirk, clearly expecting Myung-soo to be astonished by her revelation.

"But there *were* sick people," he said, treading water cautiously. "They showed them on the Newscans. Millions of them."

"That part was true," the woman said. "The government shipped the sick here under the pretext of caring for them. What they were doing was secretly infecting them. Spreading experimental strains. The doctors and the corporations – they were all part of it."

Myung-soo's skepticism must have shown, because the woman continued, impassioned now. "I was like you. It was the furthest thing from my mind. My work here was for the benefit of humanity. But that was before I heard the Prophet speak."

"The Prophet?"

"He saw through it all." The strained, weary lines of her face had relaxed into an expression of beatific ecstasy. "He was one of us too, at first. But he had the courage to stand up in defense of the truth. With that truth came empowerment."

She motioned at the windows, toward the gymnasium floor below, where a podium was being assembled. Myung-soo saw a commotion at the entrance as the captives were led inside, then to rows of chairs at the front of the assembly. No one resisted, no one was struck, or shoved, or strong-armed. Yet there was an air of coercion around the proceedings, hidden under a thin veneer of politeness: the armed side keeping a respectful distance, the captives keeping their eyes down, shuffling in obediently.

"But that means the disease is still here," Myung-soo ventured. He had once worked on a spread about a sect of religious zealots in the city, the Sunbeam Church, and he recognized the same inflections in the woman's voice. The tone that came off as calm and rational on the surface, but was never more than a hairsbreadth away from a raging diatribe. "Or are you saying—"

"The Prophet cured it." A radiant, wet-eyed smile suffused the official's plain features, an inward blossoming that for a moment made her look like a different person altogether. "With prayer, and meditation, and the strength of collective positive thinking."

She got out from behind her desk, walked a stunned Myung-soo to the door to her office. "I know it's too much to take in at once," she said. "We do not force our beliefs on outsiders here. There is no need for that. All I ask – all the Prophet asks – is that you keep your eyes and your mind open. That you allow yourself to *see*."

Could it be true? Myung-soo's thoughts were in turmoil as they walked back down the stairs, into the makeshift auditorium, the murmur of the gathered crowd vibrating the walls. The hopeful picture the woman had painted for him did not account for the corpses on the fence, or the people imprisoned in the warehouse, or the signs of disease he had encountered on the way into the camp. But there were people here, and most of them seemed to be free from the virus. He had tapped into something larger than himself here. The thought filled him with exhilaration.

Who was he to question a miracle?

It looked like the whole camp had turned up for the prayer, or speech, or whatever was about to happen. All the chairs were occupied, and people were squeezed tight against the walls, pushing toward the little stage around which a motley band of guards struggled to keep a shaky boundary. The walls picked up the noise, carried it up to the metal roof, which threw it back down at the floor, multiplied severalfold.

Pretending to take photos, Myung-soo studied the faces in the crowd. They were dirty, unkempt, and emaciated, but happy, chattering to one another, laughing, like participants in a festival. Music piped up from enormous speakers, a bland, flat melody, accompanied by a rhythmic chanting.

Myung-soo sought the woman official, but she was lost in rapture, humming or singing along with the rest of the faithful, swaying in place. Behind the podium, a wooden enclosure had been put up, surrounded by guards with spears and machetes. He zoomed in until he could make out the shadowy figures within: a few surviving scientists from the train, bruised and rumpled, looking out through the slats in trembling apprehension.

He was skirting the edge of the crowd, trying to find a better vantage point for his camera, when the lights dimmed and the mass of bodies surged forward, almost knocking him off his feet. At the far side of the hall, a man was ascending the podium. Crude as the great mural had been, Myung-soo recognized the thin features, the broad forehead, and the prominent widow's peak. Arms reached for the Prophet, groping the air. In the front row, the captives cringed and huddled together instinctively. Hunkered down behind a speaker, safely away from the frenzied throng, Myung-soo captured it all.

In his viewfinder, the Prophet raised his arms, waited for the din to die down.

"Tonight, we welcome new brothers and sisters into our midst." His voice sailed over the silent, rapturous heads, deep and hypnotic. "They brought us provisions to nourish our bodies. Most importantly, they brought the train that will carry us to fulfill our holy purpose." The Prophet paused until the applause dissipated. "If any of you had doubt or uncertainty in your hearts, doubt no more. Blessed Divinity rewards us for our patience and devotion. For our sacrifice."

"Blight on the outsiders," shouted a voice from the crowd. The Prophet mopped beads of sweat from his forehead, gestured in mild reprimand.

"All are accepted here who will believe the truth," he said. "It is our duty to bring hope to those as suffering and lost as we once were. Many of us were sent to this place to die. Cast out behind walls, behind razor wire and machineguns. Thrown into mass graves. Condemned by devils, by devious manipulators, by those who even in this direst of moments saw in us not human beings, but an opportunity to squeeze out an extra morsel of profit."

Howling, the mass rushed forward, scattering the security, overturning the chairs, in a frenzy to reach the speaker. The Prophet seemed to anticipate this. He knelt at the edge of the stage, giving himself up to his devotees. His hands touched, caressed, blessed. They raised a pale, sunken face by the chin, wiped the blood from the corners of its mouth. *Come forth*, his voice boomed from the now-awakened speakers. *Come forth and be healed.* It reminded Myung-soo of the *waeguk-saram* lay preachers he'd seen on foreign 'casts.

Caught between horror and the first stirrings of religious euphoria, the photographer watched the foremost ranks of the crowd dissolve into a frenzied melee. Had his hustle for those morsels of profit blinded him to a higher message, a genuine miracle? They were sick, those nearest the stage, blood crusted around their mouths and noses, the fever-heat radiating from their glassy eyes. But here they were, mixing with the others, spreading microscopic killers through the air, touching and kissing the hands of their savior.

Myung-soo felt himself in the grip of a greater power. For a moment, he allowed himself to believe that the sick would be healed and the dying brought back from the brink of death. He had come in for a scoop, and he was about to witness something far greater. The skeptical part of him had gone silent. Lowering his camera, he gazed at the podium, his heart filling with something akin to love for the divine deliverer.

"Saved!" The cry exploded over the sea of upraised arms, echoed through the hall. "But let us not forget the past, in this moment of triumph. Brothers and sisters, there are still those among us who refuse to see the error of their ways. Who, in their greed and hubris, thought they could use you like playthings. Who abused your bodies and tried to possess your souls. But tell me, brothers and sisters, did they succeed? Now that you have been healed by the Light, will you still let their insidious lies cloud your minds?"

"*No!*" The crowd roared as one, breathed as one, faces indistinguishable from one another. An unfocused growl welled up from the back rows, rolled over the floor like a wave, shaking the windows in their frames.

"No." The Prophet closed his eyes, held a hand up to his temple. His voice was low now, but somehow seemed to carry farther. "Because we have outsmarted them. Soon those who sent us out to die will feel the flames of our rage. The evil they brewed will consume their shining cities and their towers of arrogance."

He paused for effect, stabbed an accusing finger at the enclosure at the back of the hall. "I ask you today," he said, nodding his head slowly, "what are the wages of sin, of unforgivable sin? The punishment for the betrayal of your fellow man?"

"*Death!*" the crowd intoned, a single voice shuddering with insane fury.

"Death!" the Prophet roared, his voice echoing up the walls, down from the ceiling.

Blades gleamed in the floodlights as the screaming scientists were hauled out of their cage, knives and spears stabbing into flesh even as they walked, or crawled, or cowered through the gauntlet. Even the guards from the entrance had abandoned their posts to join in the bloody revelry. The crowd pushed closer in its madness, those without weapons kicking, or clawing, or tearing into the tortured bodies with their teeth.

Myung-soo fled for the unguarded door.

He had not run since childhood, had never taken regular exercise, and after what seemed like a very short distance his lungs were spasming, his legs burning, the stars wheeling overhead. Still he kept going, his mind darkening, his one thought to get away from the pandemonium in the assembly hall, away from the twisted, fanatical faces within. Worst of all, he had almost been swept up by the collective derangement, moments away from flinging himself headfirst into the mob. He had to get away. All thoughts of a payday had evaporated like water on a hot stone. He had to warn the outside world of the madness brewing in the camp. Otherwise there would be nowhere to escape to.

Hands gripped him from the shadows, pulled him out of the reach of the lights. Myung-soo mewled and struggled weakly, but to no avail. His captor shoved him against a wall, clamped a hand over his mouth.

"Be quiet." It was one of the voices from the warehouse – a bald, stout man whose round face shone like a frightened moon in the dark. "We spoke earlier. You're one of those who came on the train."

He peered round the corner, removed his palm from Myung-soo's lips. "We're getting out," he said, breathing hard from the exertion. "You should come with us. Tonight may be the only chance we get."

Myung-soo shook the man's hands off his shoulders. "What the hell is going on here?"

"Come." The round man listened to the howls from the gymnasium for a moment, then raced across the illuminated ground with surprising agility. "My name is Hong. I'm the camp's chief maintenance officer. Or was, before things fell apart."

He pulled Myung-soo behind an overflowing construction dumpster, held a finger up to his lips. Hurried footsteps approached and receded. Another glance, another sprint, until they reached the unlit section of the camp. Hong seemed to know every shadowy spot, every hole in the inner fencing. They crawled through a gap and lay on their stomachs, pressed tight against the cold, moist ground. When Hong deemed that the danger had passed, the two men climbed over an earth embankment and slid on all fours into some sort of concrete canal.

"Four months ago, the supply trains stopped coming." Hong's voice, disembodied in the near-total darkness, swirled around Myung-soo's ears. "The camp was already at critical capacity. More and more infected being brought in, the food stores all but empty, drinking water running low. There were rumors that the government was ready to pull the plug on the whole project. Outside of the camp, the numbers of the infected were going down. They were willing to let the problem sort itself out."

"That's monstrous," Myung-soo said. He heard, rather than saw, the other man shrug.

"It was chaos back in the city," he said. "The politicians were already in hot water over their handling of the pandemic. The journals, the Newscans, kept the pressure up on them, scandal after scandal. All paid propaganda by the pharma *chaebols*, who were vying to get their foot in the door by accusing the government of incompetence and corruption. You know how it was."

Myung-soo nodded guiltily. He had contributed some of those inflammatory articles himself, spent hours trolling social media forums, picking on targets. In spite of the danger he was in, his hunger for his story had not abated entirely. His fingers itched to snap a few quick shots of the grim faces around him, to spin them into the scoop of the decade.

"Soon the food ran out," Hong said, walking through a patch of moonlight. "Then the medicine. We couldn't bury the dead fast enough. Our own staff among them – we'd run out of protective equipment weeks ago. There were shooting incidents. Cannibalism. It was hell."

"What about the soldiers?"

"Most of them were given orders to retreat. When the mutiny broke out, those who stayed threw their lot in with the man calling himself the Prophet. He was nobody special. Just a very ill patient who recovered after the doctors had already given up on him. He convinced them that the disease is a hoax, that the only way to a cure was killing the perpetrators. Blood atonement. The few of us who tried to talk the staff out of this madness were locked up. I tried to alert the authorities before the Prophet's followers disabled all communication, but no one was answering the phones anymore."

"So the patients aren't cured," Myung-soo said. "They just believe they are."

"Everyone in this camp is still infected." Hong shook his head, a horrified expression on his face. "The last batch of drugs slowed the progression of the disease. Some of us are taking longer to develop symptoms than others. But we're all carriers at this point. Without medical help, we'll die."

Dread rolled through Myung-soo in a queasy wave as he remembered the corpses on the fence, "How can anyone believe nonsense like that, when people are still dying?" he said.

"Because the only other choice was to accept death," Hong said quietly. "Because despair had made them insane. Or because they needed to believe something. To us, it makes no difference. After tonight, the Prophet has no more use for us. The guards aren't watching us closely. That's why we were able to escape."

Myung-soo realized that he could see his surroundings. They were almost underneath the train platform, lights blazing above them, drawing long shadows from the concrete support pillars. He finally managed to fish out a coherent question from the muddy churn of his thoughts. "Why did they lure us here?" he said, stumbling behind his guide. "What do they need the train for?"

"They want to take it back to the city," Hong said, grave-faced. "To spread the disease. Don't you see? No one knows that the camp has been taken over. By the time the train is stopped at the first checkpoint, the infected will have spread everywhere. The Prophet has already assigned people to specific targets. Train and bus stations, malls, airports. Even the Naro Suborbital Terminal, if they can get through."

Myung-soo realized that his mouth was hanging open. He thought of the teeming millions behind the wall, unaware of the viral bomb heading their way. A plague to end all plagues, silently spread through an unsuspecting population. His throat constricted at the vision of the dead in the streets, heaped into mobile incinerators.

"It's not as crazy as it sounds." Hong's voice was down to a whisper as he listened for movement on the platform above. "The Prophet may have fooled those around him, but he knows the clock is ticking. His faithful are still dropping like flies around him. He also believes that a cure has already been developed. That the medical-industrial complex is withholding it for profit. By bringing the disease into the big hubs, he'll be able to strong-arm the corporations into releasing this cure. Or so he thinks."

"What if he's wrong?"

"Then it becomes their revenge," Hong said. "One last act of hate toward the world that abandoned them."

The two men were at the bottom of the platform steps. Hong raised his arm, lowered it as more figures appeared from the unlit back rooms of the station.

"Any luck?" he asked a woman in stained overalls. She shook her head. "We couldn't get close enough to the coils to disable them," she said. "There are guards posted all over the place. They have guns."

"What about the guideway?"

"We tried to damage them," said a younger man, his hands and clothes black with grime. "It was no good. You need explosives to damage the structure."

"That leaves only the switches," Hong said with finality. He turned to Myung-soo, pointed at the camera around the photographer's neck. "If we fail to stop the train from leaving, you're our last resort."

"Me?" Myung-soo stared at the engineer, then at the others, waiting for someone to let him in on the joke. "What do you think I can do?"

"Send a message." Hong's mouth was set in lines of grim authority. "There are villages to the south of this camp. Tell the authorities what's happening here. Show them the pictures you took. Tell them they have to destroy the train. Don't let it come near the city."

"Why don't you all come with me?" the photographer said. "If the Prophet's people find you, you're as good as dead."

"Our path ends here," Hong said, to murmured agreement. "You still have a chance of not being infected. But we're all carrying the disease. There's no going back for any of us."

He nodded at his team. "They'll draw the guards toward the front of the train. Give me some time to disable the switch. You crawl under the track, then head left along the wall, until you find a metal door. It's unlocked. Once you're on the other side, head straight across the field. Keep the station lights to your back. If all goes well, you'll reach the nearest settlement by morning."

Myung-soo wanted to protest, but the saboteurs were already racing up the stairs, pulling him along with them before he could utter a word. Shouts echoed under the tin roof of the station, followed by rifle shots, so loud that Myung-soo was momentarily deafened and disoriented. Then the bright lights along the tracks cut out, sinking the platform into darkness.

"That way," someone spoke in his ear. Hands pushed him down roughly – he could no longer tell whose hands – and he loped toward the edge of the platform in a clumsy half-crouch, seeing the guards' flashlights come on, their beams scything across the concrete.

He dropped down to the gravel of the guideway, scraping his elbows and knees. Pressed himself against the oily flank of the traincar and closed his eyes as boots thumped above him and voices called out orders. Lowering himself to his belly, he crawled under the car, groping blind toward the other side, aware of the tons of metal suspended over him. As soon as he was through, he got up and ran. The lights were coming back on and bullets cracked around him, but none found its mark. Here was the door, opening like Hong had said it would, and then he was through, barely aware of his actions, the sky and the fields opening up around him, a vast emptiness silvered by moonlight.

For a while he could still hear the gunshots, but gradually the lights of the camp faded into the distance, and he walked in silence, alone under the stars, dry grass rustling under his feet.

Two peasants found him a little after dawn, face down in an irrigation canal, lapping water like a dog.

When he looked up, he saw the fear in their faces. He wanted to tell them that he needed help, that lives were at stake. But his throat was swollen, his voice an inhuman croak, and the sun's first rays hurt his eyes, making them feel like they'd been rubbed with ground glass. Every muscle in his body hurt and the heat beat down on him, unbearable, cooking him alive. A furnace outside and a furnace in, charring his thoughts before he could grab hold of them. By the time he managed to raise himself to his feet, all he could see of the men were their rag-clad backs, vanishing into a copse of trees.

Groggily he followed them. There was a message he was supposed to convey – that much he remembered. Something about a train and the city and a sickness. Perhaps it was he who was sick. He certainly felt like it. But when he tried to dig deeper and remember the message, images assailed him, apocalyptic images of butchered bodies strung up on barbed wire, pecked at by flocks of black birds. Horrified, he pushed the images away, and the meaning was gone with them.

After some time – maybe hours, maybe days – he found himself on the outskirts of a settlement. The houses looked empty and ill-kept, the windows missing, warnings and military signposts hammered into the walls. HAZMAT DISPOSAL, one read, and another QUARANTINE AREA. Dully he grasped what the signs were meant to convey, but there was nowhere else to go. The signs were old, anyway: some hung crooked, while others had been ripped off and lay in the dust. The vandalism didn't concern him much. He needed more water. An incredible thirst parched him, and his body was on fire. He saw his breath come out as flames, and realized he was hallucinating.

There were so many houses to choose from, the doors either open, or missing altogether. He entered the nearest one, paused in the gloomy entryway, still littered with dusty shoes, staring at the empty living room. It wasn't much, but he would be alone here, unbothered. He collapsed on the couch, the resulting dust cloud setting off a coughing fit. Myung-soo coughed long and hard, a horrible hacking, rending sensation in his chest, a bolt of pain. He leaned forward and spat red all over the floor and the broken side table. It didn't matter. He could explain it all later when the family who lived here came back.

His bloody lips worked soundlessly. In a lucid flash, the shoes had reminded him of why he'd come to the village. People. The virus. Quarantine. There might still be time to stop the worst from happening.

He set up his camera on the table, propping it up with a pair of books. The light wouldn't come on, a piece was hanging off the side, and no matter how he adjusted the lens the view-finder remained black, the network icon blinking NO CON-NECTION. But this was his big scoop, and he intended to seize it. He could already hear the bank deposit notifications pinging in. Inside the silent house, Myung-soo took a struggling breath, gazed directly into the dead camera, and began to speak.

SPOOK

Nothing felt as good as killing did. The ultimate stimulant, the grand unspeakable act that cleared the neural cobwebs and got the brain firing full throttle.

From the fearful body language of the Big Man's assistant, Tranh had inferred that he was smiling and wired with excitement. His smile tended to unnerve people – just the way he liked it. Vatgrown spies-for-hire who spent most of their lives hibernating in low-earth orbit tended to make the help nervous, regardless of what team they were currently playing for. Tranh was well aware of this as he turned his borrowed face to the myriad surveillance cameras.

In the thirty-four minutes it took the skimmer to reach the PLG arcology, he had gotten the basics of his assignment down. He had memorized the dozen or so faces, biodata, and sublimated intelligence files. Now all that was left was the meeting with his employer, or at least the face his employer put forward to the world. It had been almost a year since he'd last been decanted, and the world shimmered with a slight dissonance, a faint but persistent sense of being half a step behind, as if reality were a thin layer of cellophane that might peel any moment, revealing something altogether different. Tranh felt a wild exuberance, his hands clenching and unclenching in his pockets.

The Big Man –Chief Special Initiatives Officer, read the placard on his office door – was all perfect teeth and hair, fashionable muscles on a lean, tanned frame. He was handpicked from the corporate creche, as tailored for his position as his immaculate three-piece suit.

"Very happy to have you here," he said, pumping Tranh's hand. "Your references are impeccable. Of course, we expected no less from a trade house as storied as yours. It gives us confidence that the matter will be handled with the utmost care and delicacy."

"Glad to hear that, sir." Tranh was immediately alert with his hidden senses picking up pheromones in the other man's sweat and interpreting the tiny flicks of his eyes. Behind the polished surface and the affable manner, the Big Man was a wreck: the gleam of sweat at his hairline and the dilation of his pupils suggested as much. He had popped a trank less than half an hour ago, but the glaze of ice in his bloodstream couldn't quite conceal the hormonal storm raging inside it.

Personal agendas and motivations did not usually factor into Tranh's equation. Loyalties came and went like the seasons. Corporate ideologies bored him. But unstable people were invariably a risk to an operation, and the Big Man, as much as he'd like to convince Tranh otherwise, was one such element.

"It should be a straightforward extraction job," the Chief said. "Mid-exec level, high talent and potential. Our insiders have identified a defector in Sloane Global Capital. The situation looks promising but the target wants guarantees."

"I see." It didn't quite fit together with what Tranh had assimilated from the files. The specs had suggested a more straightforward and permanent solution for dealing with the opposition executive. But the change in tack was hardly surprising. These C-suite types never gave you the full picture. Perhaps they'd changed their mind or managed to negotiate with the target. "Extractions are not my specialty, or that of my House. But rest assured, we can accommodate the request."

"Naturally." The Chief did his best to look calm and collected. "We have an in-house extraction team. But this is a sensitive matter. Pacific can't be implicated, and deniability is our paramount concern. You'll be there to see that it goes off smoothly."

It was unusual to see a *gweilo*, a white devil, in charge of black ops for the second biggest asset management conglomerate in the Dragon Republic, working under the scrutiny of the Board as well as the unfaltering gazes of the government Cadres. Then again, maybe it made more sense than Tranh thought. His impressive title notwithstanding, the Chief was an outsider, therefore probably a figurehead. If something went wrong, someone would have to take the heat, and the conglomerate would serve the *gweilo* to the Cadres on a silver platter. Now the Chief wanted a third party to deflect the blame onto, and who better than a faceless hired gun already on his way back to orbit? That way the Chief got to keep his plush, airconditioned office, which beat the alternative: a gray jumpsuit and hard labor in a reclamation colony.

"I'm afraid I'm not following," Tranh said. He understood exactly what was going on, but the white lie offered the Chief a face-saving excuse. "Perhaps it would help if I had the complete file."

"It's being transmitted as we speak." The Chief looked almost smug, oblivious to his gaffe. No wonder the Cadres tolerated this overfed, overconfident Westerner, for all his obvious shortcomings. Easy to manipulate with a smile and a nod, easier still to be made to disappear, another arcology-bred *gweilo* seamlessly filling his chair, like an illusionist's trick.

"My cover has presumably already been established."

The Big Man slid an ident card across the polished surface of his desk. "You are a merger specialist," he said, surrounding his words with air quotes. "Hired by one of our shell companies to negotiate a deal for a chain of factories in the Northern Mediterranean."

Tranh glanced at the holoprint on the card. He liked his new face better than his current one.

"Most of the background work is done," the Chief said, taking Tranh's silence for agreement. "The target is committed. We don't expect any trouble. But it is good to prepare for contingencies. I take it you have your bases covered in case your cover is blown."

Tranh restrained himself to a small nod, letting slide the offensive implication about his lack of preparedness. "What about the rest of my negotiation team? Are they part of the operation?"

"They know nothing." An offhand wave. "Expendable. Do not concern yourself with anyone but your target. If the team gets in your way, you are free to do as you wish."

The Big Man smiled, extended a tanned hand across the table. Tranh accepted the hand, shook it with just the right amount of tension.

"Understood," he said. "It is a pleasure."

He meant every word of it.

After the treatments, administered by a sallow-skinned doctor in a secretly repurposed government euthanasia clinic, Tranh got a room at a seafront highrise hotel and spent a week recovering. Autosurgeons had subtly altered the contours of his face and tinted his eyes and hair. A diet of starchy carbohydrates, combined with insulin suppressors, thickened his trim to middle-aged respectability, enhancing his hibernation bloat. He now looked vaguely Eurasian, another one of the overworked, underslept, and badly dressed drones milling about corporate offices all along the Digital Coast.

Tranh enjoyed his new pudgy self, the heft of his torso and limbs, the sweaty, oppressive embrace of gravity. The decanting hangover had almost dispersed, the hibernation nightmares fleeing from the sunlight, leaving him with a rollercoaster of unfamiliar emotions and urges he could now explore at will, with the wonderment of a child. His fractured personality took to its new mold like a fish to water.

As he waited for his hormone levels to balance out, he took long walks outside. Dusk was his favorite time: roads spread like a web centered on the gleaming sprawl of the city, the dark bulk of the Yanshan-Pudong seawall in the distance, the vast heaving sea. Dim shapes protruded from the waves, the sunken domes and towers of Old Shanghai, islands of patchwork construction proliferating around them in defiance of the elements. Rumor had it that many of the city's poor still inhabited the above-surface floors refusing to give up.

The scrabble of human vermin to survive never ceased to amaze Tranh. All it would take was a tectonic tremor, or another polar ice shelf melting, and the bay would rise up to swallow all that pointless effort. But people carried on and people built again, and every disaster only strengthened their resolve, even when life meant nothing but more suffering. To Tranh, their behavior reflected the tenacity of the Dragon Republic itself. It was the last government still setting its own rules, not just serving as stage dressing for the transnationals: a plodding but invulnerable leviathan weathering storm after storm.

It was especially good to be around crowds so he could immerse himself into the boil and hustle of humanity. Perhaps he would become a part of it someday and leave his past behind like a discarded set of clothes. He might lie low and prey on the human herd from the anonymity of its ranks. One or two at a time when the old blood-hunger was on him, picking off the weak and isolated. The thought made him almost giddy with happiness.

Upper Kowloon was a patchwork of glass towers rising from the water, their ferroconcrete feet firmly planted in the ocean bed below, crisscrossed by a cat's cradle of bridges and moveways suspended above the waves. Miles out to the sea, not a trace of the old city was visible. In a few decades, the water will rise and the arcologies will retreat further inland, leaving the golden towers to drown. Right now, it was the trade nexus of the coast, a free enterprise zone facilitating exchange with the rest of Panasia, far enough from the Dragon to escape its smoldering jaws, but close enough to feel the heat of its breath.

The delegation flew into the floating airport and emerged in a geodesic dome aflutter with corporate and national banners. Spies of all stripes slunk through its hallways, along with the usual smattering of poorly disguised, bleary-eyed apparatchiks. A Single-Entry Commercial Visitor's Visa, purchased with anonymous cryptokuai, saw Tranh through immigration unmolested. He nodded politely to the plainclothes thug assigned to the delegation by the Directorate of the Interior, and both sides went through the motions, assuming the expected roles of follower and followed, all the way to the arcology. There the Sloane corpmercs took over, and the Directorate man pocketed his bribe to elide the lengthy and largely ceremonial sign-in protocols. Tranh joined the others for a light supper, then secluded himself in his room, rolled down the shutters, and played back the case file in his head.

Lu Huiyin, the defector, had entered Sloane as an outsider, and risen through the rigid corporate hierarchy with the speed of a suborbital shuttle. Despite its foreign name, appended as a result of an acquisition, Sloane was still very much an old-fashioned *jituan* in every sense that mattered. The heavy hand of the Party had molded Sloane's mentality for close to half a century, and even in the so-called liberated atmosphere of post-Emergence deregulation, the company clung to its outdated structures like a drunk to a lamppost.

One among millions of overly bright New Cadres produced by the Republic's business management mills, Lu Huiyin had caught the eye of the previous management through an uncanny combination of intelligence and intuition. Unfortunately for her, the same talents that had propelled her meteoric ascent had also earned her the enmity of the company's more conservative *laobans*. Her shrewd nose for asset-stripping opportunities had failed her when it came to picking sides in the boardroom wars. Subtly frozen out and sidelined, she saw her projects passed over and her requests for more operational funding falling on deaf ears. Yet Sloane refused to let her go and her contract was ironclad. The new Board was content to keep paying her without letting her work and wait for the clock to run out on her employment.

Pacific Logistics was interested in what she had to offer and was willing to extend a generous compensation package and fast track to the senior executive level. Tranh was to secure formal commitment and whisk the expert away from under the noses of Sloane's security. It sounded a little too neat and clean, but he didn't let it worry him. If wrinkles came up, he would smooth them out which was precisely what he was looking forward to doing.

His negotiation team was treated with customary deference, but largely ignored. Several other delegations were housed in the same wing of the arcology, including a stern-looking, buttoned-up set of Cadres from the Directorate of Transition Initiatives, who paraded up and down the central concourse,

palmers at the ready, keeping their eyes peeled for any ideo-
logical blasphemy or controversial marketing slogan. Tranh's
team trailed in the wake of the Cadres' righteous bluster, unnoticed and almost despondent, sending out meeting requests
that went unanswered, spending long idle hours at the cafes
and restaurants. Nor were they the only ones shunned: Tranh's
facial recognition wetware picked out at least one other party
of visitors in a similar predicament, cheap Mainland suits and
plastic ident tags signaling their outsider status, adrift in benevolent neglect. He sidled closer to this group of fellow pariahs
with a look of bored indifference on his face, and homed in his
aural augments on the strands of conversation drifting through
the background noise.

One of the women in the group caught his gaze and
offered a small, inviting smile. Tall and long-limbed, with short
black hair and generically pretty features, she sidled closer to
Tranh, one arm slung over the backrest.

"Welcome to the waiting room," she said, with a wry
chuckle. "Really, they should just assign us numbered tickets
and call out our names. But this place is all about politeness.
No client is too small, and all that."

"Are you ahead of us in line, or behind?"

"Doesn't matter. If you're staying on this level, you're
strictly third-tier. You're not getting what you came here for.
Might as well make the most of the free food and booze." She
raised her cocktail glass, indicated the rest of Tranh's team
already getting rowdy in the next booth. "I suppose life could
be worse."

"I don't know. Is there a fourth tier?"

That got him a laugh, one louder than he thought was
strictly merited. "I'm Klara," the woman said, searching his
face with her eyes. Tranh responded with the name on his new
ident card. She named the outfit she was with, a minor risk
management player he had vaguely heard of. "Sloane's botan-
ical gardens are among the chief sights of the coast," she said.
"Something like half its trees are extinct elsewhere. Have you
been up to their Seaview Terrace?"

"Can't say that I have." Tranh pegged her for a junior team member, bored out of her mind and eager to impress, looking for a way to kill time.

"We should meet there for drinks," she said, her hand brushing his wrist. "If you're not working evenings, of course."

She was flirting with him, Tranh realized, genuinely confused for the first time in as long as he could remember. He heard himself utter a few equally meaningless responses, felt his facial muscles grow taut in a smile.

Tranh made all the right responses but remained noncommittal as they parted. Maybe the girl was bait sent to test him, or maybe she was a free spirit with nothing to hide. Either way, the uncertainty was mildly exciting. It was part of that great unknown, the human experience, that had eluded him for so long.

In the semidarkness of his room, he removed his clothes and lay on the bed, fantasizing about Klara. Stepping out of the shadows behind her, silent as a wraith, wrapping his hands around her shapely neck. The malleable feel of her trachea under his fingers, crushed like a thin copper pipe. Her vertebrae snapping with a dry, brittle crack. Watching the life fade out of her cellgen green eyes. As the joy of the release flooded his system, Tranh submerged himself into sleep, a blissful smile on his lips, his hand squeezing the sheets.

There were bureaucratic functions to attend – the signing of non-disclosure agreements in triplicate, the poring over stiff boilerplate language drafted a generation ago – and miles of red tape to go through, the fading pomp and circumstance from a bygone era that even the Party no longer remembered the purpose of. Negotiations commenced, halted, and resumed under the bleary eyes of hungover and heavily bribed Cadres. Somewhere between this meaningless briefing and that drawn-out compliance review, Tranh managed to sequester Lu Huiyin and exchange the prearranged codes. He was out of practice with extractions, and he expected to have to soothe nerves, to encourage and cajole, offer assurances and reassurances. If the plan failed, if the extraction had to be aborted, he harbored no illusions about the fate awaiting him or his target. But Lu Huiyin was calm, businesslike, as if it were someone else's life on the line.

"I trust everything is ready for our little jaunt," she said during a smoking break, watching the argument in the conference room from a safe distance, the rival teams heating up over a contract clause here, a figure there. "How long until we leave?"

Tranh knew better than to overpromise. He had already mapped the potential escape routes, replaying them in his head over and over. Adding details and small corrections based on what he'd observed such as synchronizing their movements with the security patrols and evading likely choke points. One option was to sneak out through the arcology's belowground service levels. Another one was a daring dash across the unfinished portion of the rail-shuttle line. If everything else failed, he'd dump a corpse to misdirect pursuit. It was an appealing notion, in every respect. Either way, their timing had to be impeccable.

"Three days," he said. "Maybe four. But I have to know you're ready. There can't be any second-guessing."

"I'm ready," she said. They spoke without looking at each other, standing out on the glassed-in loggia, the sea glittering with afternoon gold beyond a cascade of mirrored residential quarters. "I've been ready for a while. Staying here is a losing proposition. Sloane is too tied up with the Party to stay ahead of the times. The Comrades think they can keep a tight lid on the capital market, but they're only delaying the inevitable."

"You came up through the same system," Tranh said. "What made you change your mind?"

Lu Huiyin didn't so much as blink. "The world is a different place," she said. "Modern industry belongs in the orbitals. Better efficiency, vacuum storage, endless waste-dumping capacity. Sloane's heading for a cliff, but they refuse to abandon the Party line. Serving two masters rarely works well for very long. I don't want to be around when the inevitable happens."

Tranh nodded. She seemed to be speaking from the heart. "It's an old civilization," he said.

"You sound like an admirer."

"Only a fool underestimates a powerful opponent." Tranh smiled and bowed his head slightly. "Naturally, the market will always seek to balance itself out."

"Naturally." Lu Huiyin's face was expressionless again, as if a shutter had fallen over it. "It's best for us not to be seen together again," she said, walking slowly toward the glass entrance doors. "There are no listening devices out here, but the security AIs track movement patterns. Anything longer than a couple of minutes, and our meeting will be flagged."

"By the Cadres?"

"The Cadres couldn't find their own behind with a map. It's Sloane. Our corpmercs have been placed on high alert. They're suspecting infiltration by outside agents. What about the others on your team?"

The spy shook his head. "Expendable," he said. "No loose ends if I can help it."

"Now is a good time to start tying them up." She leaned over the parapet, speaking over her shoulder. "Make sure we leave in the next day or two. Any later and we start pushing our luck."

Later that day he met Klara for drinks at the rooftop bar. Other than as an object to slake his killing thirst, he felt no interest in her, either conversational or sexual, but she would provide a welcome cover. His heightened senses had spotted a pair of hard-faced plainclothes security guards posing as a couple near the doors Another lurker by the polished wooden counter pretending to nurse a drink. Likely corporate counter-intelligence either marking a threat or keeping an eye on the general situation. Lu Huiyin's warning was right.

Tranh ordered drinks and slipped into his mask as a lonely salaryman making a clumsy pass at a pretty young girl he'd met on a work trip. None of the corpmercs batted an eyelid as he crossed to Klara's table, taking great care not to spill the contents of the two glasses.

She smiled at him and twirled her empty wine glass. "I hope your day is going better than mine."

"It's certainly starting to look up," Tranh said. It seemed like the right thing to say. "What can we do to make yours better?"

She sighed with an exaggerated roll of her eyes. "Get me out of this place, for a start. Paperwork's a killer and the government officials are pigs. You don't want to sit next to one of them while wearing a skirt."

Tranh set the drinks down carefully, nodded at the sunset. "It's hard to think about work with a view like this."

"Poison." Klara giggled as he gaped at her "That's what makes it so beautiful. Chemical pollution in the air. It kills the elderly and causes birth defects in babies. But from up here, it's magnificent. Enchanting."

He nodded vaguely and took a sip of his cocktail. Alcohol never sat well with him. He could never predict how it would interact with his adrenal enhancers, but he had a transdermal in his room that would mitigate the worst of the side effects. A small price to pay for blending in. "I take it your work here is done?" he said, watching her over the rim of his glass.

"In a manner of speaking. We're being forced to tender, rather than signing immediately, as expected. Sloane's negotiators drive a hard bargain. But I'd rather not talk about work tonight."

Klara raised her glass in a toast. Her amused eyes studied him slowly. "You don't give away much, do you?" she said, waving at the waiter.

Tranh reached for her hand under the table and leaned closer.

Klara flinched, a frisson of fear clouding her dark eyes. Tranh realized that his grin had become too wide and fixed, that he was squeezing her hand hard enough to feel the small bones inside. With some difficulty, he reined in his bloodlust. "A true professional never tells," he said, lowering his voice to the appropriate seductive timbre. "Discretion is written into my non-disclosure agreement."

"Non-disclosure suits me fine."

They talked awhile longer, letting the tension between them build. Tranh watched the girl closely as she spoke. Her face was flawless, delicately constructed. Her build and general likeness to Lu Huiyin were uncanny. He had not recognized it before, but she could be the diversion he was looking for, in more ways than one. A corpse would throw the security teams off track, buy Tranh and the defector valuable time to make their escape. Especially if he smashed those porcelain features beyond recognition and left the girl inside Lu Huiyin's room, with Lu Huiyin's clothes and ident card on her. Yes. Klara fit the bill perfectly. By the time Sloane saw through the ruse, Tranh and the real Lu Huiyin would be beyond their reach.

Tranh could see that he intrigued the girl, that she was interpreting his scrutiny as sexual interest, and responding in turn. It suited him to have her believe that. He felt neither excitement nor revulsion about what lay ahead: the act itself was repetitive, bizarre, a task to be completed like any other. One step leading into the next, building up to the predictable climax, fading into the impersonal awkwardness of the aftermath. But the plan was already in place, and their tryst wouldn't get in the way. If anything, it would set the stage for the next phase, the extraction itself.

Besides, there were far worse ways to kill a few hours.

Buzzing with pleasant anticipation of the impending kill, Tranh signaled for the check, and allowed himself to be led back to the visitors' quarters.

Footsteps stirred him from light sleep. They were distant but not silent enough for his enhanced senses. Sloane security had worked it all out. They always did, somehow – but if Tranh wasn't ready, he'd been at this game too long to be caught flat-footed.

He waited for the first corpmerc to charge through the door, leaped on the man, broke his neck with a quick twist, and was already rolling toward the bed when the other two opened fire. His mattress absorbed the concussive blast from their stungel shotguns as he rushed them from the dark room, knocking them to the floor and pinning them confused and deaf under their ear protectors. He punched the closer one in the throat, disabling him, then flipped the mattress, picked up a shotgun, and fired into the other. At point-blank range, the guard's face caved into a bloody bowl.

The subsonic bang was still rattling the doors in their frames as Tranh raced down the corridor, setting off fire alarms as he went. He signaled Lu Huiyin to get moving and broke into the fire escape, racing down the illuminated staircases and listening for heavy bootsteps under the riptide of spreading panic.

An entire team was waiting outside the elevators, and these ones did not believe in nonlethal force. Tranh burst out onto the gallery above, running in a low crouch as they opened fire. A fusillade of bullets shredded the awnings and pulverized the glass above the parapet. Diving behind a concrete planter, he activated his beacon device and counted off the seconds. Imagined the signal racing straight up into the thermosphere, being picked up by a satellite and relayed to an EMP-proof bunker on an uninhabited island in the South China Sea, where a neurojacked hacker was waiting, encapsulated like a virus inside Sloane's utility control systems.

When the lights went out and the elevators and walkways ground to a halt, Tranh launched himself over the edge, into the blind chaos below, landed on a manicured lawn, and kept running. In the seventy-five seconds it took for the power to be restored, he had already scuttled between the paralyzed transportation shuttles, as stealthy and sleek as a rat, and was pounding along the empty track, heading for the terminus of the line.

Something had gone wrong despite of all his preparations. Sloane's security had been tipped off. The thought burned inside him like acid, curdling his blood. But his lungs and heart kept up their smooth rhythm as the stims kicked in and his muscles responded, propelling him faster down the dark track. There had been no warning, but also no attempt to contain and isolate him: the decision had to have been made instantly. Tranh put it aside, focused on the track and the piston-like pumping of his arms and legs. All that was left was to hope that his mark had not been apprehended, that the mission was not compromised beyond salvage.

At the maintenance access, he keyed an override into the lock and hauled himself over thick bundles of pipes and conduits, through the open hatch door and onto the unfinished part of the line.

Damp, chilly air drove off the heaving sea whipping his face. A hundred or so feet below, the sandbar stretched away into the night. The rail was a single steel blade projecting like a bayonet, abruptly ending in nothingness. Huddled in the lee of a steel pillar, Tranh turned on his beacon again and sent several short bursts of narrow-beam-laser data toward the stars. He counted to ten, then transmitted three longer pulses, flung the device into the howling abyss beneath him, and waited.

A figure detached itself from the darkness further down the track and waved to him. Alarmed, Tranh glanced around for a weapon, then recognized Lu Huiyin. He crept cautiously along the slick steel beam, blinking against the spray and wind. The defector had to be far more athletic than she looked to make it all the way out there. Even with all his training, Tranh could only move a few feet at a time with his arms flung out like a tightrope walker.

Far under his feet, the sandbar vanished under the frothing sea. The structure vibrated like a tuning fork under the combined assault of the elements. It wouldn't be long now: a light flared in the dark sky, as tiny as the fading stars at first, growing steadily. Tranh thought he could hear the thrum of the skimmer's tiltjets over the wind and the waves.

The figure came to meet him, nimble amid the buffeting of the gale. A woman clad in a black jumpsuit, goggles covering her face. Closer up, Tranh could see why she moved with such confidence. There was scaling gear on her hands and feet, webbing around her waist and shoulders, fastening her to the narrow rail.

Salt spray rushed up into his face, slicking the track like ice. He drew breath to cry out a warning to Lu Huiyin, let it out in a hiss as a blast of the wind threw him off balance. For a giddy, panicked moment he was weightless, suspended above the raging sea. He spun, recovered, slipped again, clutched at the rail with both hands. He tried to right himself, but another gust made the steel shiver as if from a hammerblow. Clinging for dear life, frozen needles stabbing his eyes, Tranh silently urged the skimmer to hurry.

The woman made her way over with careful grace. One of her gecko pads was off, hanging from a slender wrist. Realization trickled slowly into Tranh's awareness as he saw the small pistol in her hand, the magnitude of his mistake.

Klara's other hand pushed the goggles off her face. She stood close enough to be heard over the wind, but well out of reach. Her aim was steady, feet spread in a shooter's stance, the pads on her soles gripping the metal.

"You should have let security take you," she said. "It would have been easier that way. Less running for everyone involved."

Tranh looked up. The transport was almost upon them, the engines whirring and shifting pitch, battling the gale. "They won't let you board without me," he said, scanning the track, trying to spot Lu Huiyin. Surely she couldn't be out here, risking her life.

Then he saw the boat, far down under the trestles, tossed on the gray waves like driftwood. Matte black, all but invisible. He laughed, a hollow, grating sound. The game had been flipped, the predator becoming the prey.

"We needed a distraction," Klara said. "The utility hit was a nice touch. Can't have been easy to arrange. But very effective. While Sloane's whole security team was chasing you, Lu Huiyin walked out right in front of everyone's noses, stepped off the executive marina pier, and was gone."

Tranh made a strangled noise and lunged for her. Barely felt the pain as the bullet clipped his knee, which was enough to send him down on all fours again.

The VTOL had settled into a circling pattern, beams searching the blackness, a figure with a winch harness hanging out the open door. Lights were coming on behind him too, molten gold pouring across the glass cliff of the arcology as the armed guards closed in.

"It doesn't have to end like this," he said, knowing it was futile. "You win. You got your mark. I'm not in your way. Just let me leave."

"I'm afraid I can't do that." The muzzle of the pistol motioned him back. "Your genetic profile is all over their databases. Isn't that what makes you so good at what you do? The perfect weapon, leaving no trace, except on a cellular level. I sampled your DNA from a glass during our first meeting but needed a little bit more to make it believable. All evidence points to you, and when they capture you, it will all add up."

Overhead, the skimmer fought the air currents, flashed its useless lights. "I could order my people to shoot you," Tranh said. "Blow up the boat, too."

"You're taking this personally." Klara glanced over the side, signaled the boat below. "It's not personal. Your employers were outbid, is all. They can try again. With someone else running the show, probably. I don't think your flying friends will let you board without your target. Might be the end of the road for you."

She squatted down, tested the rappel webbing with her free hand. "No more small talk. I can end it here, if you want me to. One bullet, and it will be over. It would beat getting captured by Sloane."

Tranh's fingers were sticks of ice. He gripped the cold metal, running desperate scenarios in his head. A shot, a long fall into the sea, then oblivion. Maybe he could take the girl with him. Before he could decide, Klara was gone, over the edge of the track. Freefalling the first twenty feet or so, then the climbing rig seized her, slowed her descent. Swinging like a pendulum, she worked her way down the line and disappeared. Tranh tried to follow the boat with his eyes, but the plumes of spray hid it for a moment, and he could not find it again.

He looked up from the precipice. The pistol was on the rail. Targeting dots swarmed over him like fireflies. Grin frozen on his face like a death mask, the spook pushed himself up and dove forward, toward the gray mirror of the water.

FREEHOLD

I was out in the sorghum fields when the news came. An unexpected, but welcome second harvest had us all pulling double shifts, taking turns washing and sleeping. At least twenty of us were hard at work, our heads bent down, muscles aching. It was a bright blue day, the sun hot on our backs, gleaming off the grain silos and water towers. Down the dirt road, a cluster of simple white buildings nestled in the green, undulating valley. Our very own paradise. Breeze sent rippling waves through the stalks, cooling our sweat, carrying the pealing of the meeting bell from the assembly hall. It never rang in the middle of the day. No one said anything, but the glances we exchanged spoke louder than words. Trouble was on the way, or already here.

Fairchild and Two-Hearts had found the fugitives near the granaries. Hiding behind the autocombines, they were rummaging through the long grass for cobs of corn that had fallen off the conveyors. The group contained two men and three women, one woman being more of a girl who was terrified and visibly pregnant. Two little ones peeking out behind the 'combine tracks, eyes as wide as their faces. They were all thin and dirty with feet blistered from days of walking on empty roads. Luckily, they were too tired to put up a fight because both Fairchild and Two-Hearts always went out armed. Our Eyes had spotted the intruders as soon as they crossed our property line and tracked them through our mapping drones. We were well prepared – or thought we were. These days it was a necessity, with the consortiums squeezing us like tweezers around a tick, with the great Midwestern dustbowl only a barometric change away, looming over us like God's own judgment.

The intruders were locked up in a tool shed by the time I arrived at the tribunal. Dawn Mother gave them food and water, although some of the members objected, worried about the agricultural consortiums' reaction if word got out. A low, annoyed muttering filled the high rafters of the converted barn. The sanded-oak floor was packed wall to wall, which meant no hands were out working in the fields in peak harvest. Darker concerns loomed unspoken: a collapsing market, a new disease, the corporations targeting our crops with an engineered strain. Landis, our Chair, sought immediately to reassure us.

"We've put them in isolation," he said, striving to keep his voice above the buzz in the hall. "Two-Hearts ran bio checks on all of them. Nothing on the rapid tests, no hits on the swabs. They're not carrying."

"Why the hell are they here, then?" Anderson's voice boomed off the rafters and the metal walls, inexplicably louder the further back he sat. "More importantly, how did they get in? It took us too long to get our act together. We have sensors and drones all over that side of the property."

"We have infrared sensors," I said. "Weed-spraying drones. This is not a military installation. Things can get through."

"Let's table the tech discussion," Landis said with a huff. He turned to Fairchild and Two-Hearts, who reflexively straightened in their seats. Both had served in the National Guard during the Water Wars out west and retained their military bearing. "You two get anything out of them?"

"Refugees from the coast," Fairchild said. "Tired old story. Lived in the Bay Area, stayed after independence. Fled for their lives after the corpmercs invaded. They had nowhere to go, just went on foot, with whatever they could carry on their backs."

"Just the five of them?" I asked. The roads were dangerous, even more so without strength in numbers, and with two children to care for.

"There were more." She shook her closely cropped head. "Most of them never made it past Six Rivers. Got into some kind of trouble with the drug cartels up there. Wouldn't say what it was. Eventually they detoured east."

"To do what?"

"They're trying to get north," Fairchild said. "To the border."

The muttering in the barn grew louder at her words. "To the border?" Landis frowned. "Did you tell them—"

"I didn't tell them shit," Fairchild snapped back. "Not in my job description. They've been on the road for months. A lot has changed since then."

"Wherever they're going, we can't let them stay here." Anderson's voice again, brooking no argument. He gazed from face to face, seeking approval, or at least agreement. Getting it from many, as far as I could see. "If the consortiums get wind of us sheltering deadbeats, they'll isolate us. The rules are clear. No charity cases."

"They will do no such thing." Dawn Mother scoffed. "We're not in breach of contract. If the consortiums won't buy from us, we have other options."

"No, we don't." Anderson's face was a dull red. Veins stood out in his neck. Stained overalls notwithstanding, it wasn't hard to imagine him as a hotshot lawyer, which was exactly what he had been before the Deregulation. "Who controls our water? Who sells us fuel for the machines? How about the roads we use to transport our products? These people have to go, and that's final."

I scanned the assembled freeholders from my sheltered spot, gauging their mood: determination, sympathy, and a lot of uncertainty. Most of us had come to this green valley, soaked by both sun and rain, to get away from having to make choices like this one. To lock ourselves away from the greed and inhumanity of the outside world. Our decision would have to be unanimous, or we might as well not bother making it.

"There are children in the group," Dawn Mother said, crossing her arms over her chest. "We can't turn them away. One of them is pregnant, for God's sake. It's not right."

"That's not our problem."

"At least let them stay until she's due. It's not against any laws."

"It isn't," Landis said in his reasonable, calm voice, "but laws don't matter anymore. Contract clauses do. Specifically, the ones covering ethical breaches. Sheltering non-consumers."

"Stop calling them that." Two-Hearts glared at Landis, then at the assembly. "They're human beings. It wasn't like they had much of a choice."

Landis turned to me, exasperated. "You're quiet. More so than usual."

I did my best to look indifferent, not to focus on any of the agitated faces. "Letting them stay is risky," I said. "They're not shareholders, and have no means to buy into the co-op. The consortiums take this sort of issue very seriously. Even if the contract doesn't hold up, we don't have the wherewithal to fight them in arbitrage."

"No one has to know," Dawn Mother said. "We'll keep them out of sight for a few months, never let them out of the shed and far from prying eyes. There's plenty of food – they won't show up on our consumer indices."

Even Anderson had to concede this point. I saw several naysayers lower their eyes, their murmur of support the lawyer dying out momentarily.

"Unless," Anderson said, "unless these people *are* the prying eyes. Unless they were sent to entrap us. We could lose everything."

"Sent by who?"

"Take your pick." Anderson snorted. "Titan, NovAgro, Singenix, Bayer-Monsanto. Every megacorp out there wants our land. They'll crush us with any chance they get. Our priority must be to keep ourselves safe."

"Put it to the vote," someone shouted in the background. "Ayes and nays. We have the right to decide."

"We're not voting on this," Landis said, but he sounded hesitant. He kept looking over at me, as if expecting me to speak up and cut through the conundrum.

I shifted in my seat, feeling the hard edges of my chair dig into the thin flesh of my buttocks. There had been a lot more padding on those parts, back in my days in the City: genehacked rice and eleven flavors of krill cakes, cheap carbohydrates and long-shelf-life triglycerides had left their mark. All that superfluous flesh had been whittled away in my first harvest season at the cooperative – working in the dirt from sunup to sundown, trying to outrace the pests and the weather, eating not by taste, or for convenience, but whatever was in season.

I came to the high plains in a year of revolutions. After the earthquake, after the floods and the fall of the government, people were afraid, and fearful people tend to turn to the known and defined. Except that the old structures they had placed their faith in were gone. I understood that, and I adapted. Life as I knew it was over, but I had contacts and connections, and a skill set that would remain in demand no matter who was running the show. While those skills made some of the freeholders wary in my presence, none of them would deny my usefulness to the commune.

The gathering quieted down. Rows and rows of sun-burned, worried faces. No one addressed me directly, but I could sense the weight of their thoughts. Bioengineered enhancement can look like magic, and sometimes it's confused for magic. I didn't need enhanced senses to realize they were expecting me to pull a rabbit out of a hat.

But I couldn't. Not without thinking about those seven human beings marched into the tool shed, the pregnant girl in front, cradling her enormous belly like a watermelon.

"Give me two days," I said, feeling the gathering's scrutiny shift to me. Two days wouldn't change a thing, but I wanted to break the tension in the room. It didn't matter, because I knew the others would believe me. Because they wanted to believe. "I'll do the best I can."

Fairchild accompanied me to the shed, cradling an old propellant shotgun. We didn't talk much. She's friendly enough to me, but I sense that my modifications make her distinctly uncomfortable. I've picked up on as much, and it doesn't bother me. On any given day, I prefer to keep my own company.

The fugitives were clustered in one corner of the prefab, not afraid, but alert. Cleaned up, fed, and dressed in borrowed clothes, they looked even thinner and more lost than before. Several of them stared at me without bothering to hide it. Most of my changes are on the inside – glands have been removed or added, organs moved around, wetware boosts slotted into living tissue. But those who meet me find my appearance disturbing, without being able to quite put their finger on why. I nodded to

Fairchild and she frowned, but left the shed, pulling the door shut behind her.

"Welcome," I said, floundering in the awkward silence that ensued. My strength is in watching from the sidelines, picking up the signs. "Did you get enough to eat? We have more food, if you're still hungry."

There was an assenting murmur from those nearest to me, but it died out quickly. "Picked the right time to come," I said, sweat prickling under my armpits. "We're in harvest season. Could do with a few extra hands in the fields."

It was a long shot – hiring vagrants is only slightly less illegal than feeding them – but they seemed to buy it. The men sat up straighter, the women nodded at me. I smiled at the children, who came up to me without fear.

Gradually I coaxed the rest to open up. Their story was consistent. One of the men, who introduced himself as James, assumed the role of speaker. "We appreciate you taking us in," he said, with a shy smile. "There aren't many folks who have been hospitable to us on the way. Or treated us like people. But we don't want to get you in trouble. We know how it is."

I nodded my agreement. "I hear you're headed up north, to the border."

"We have the little ones to think of." James gestured to the two children, then at the pregnant girl, who was asleep on a cot, exhausted. His eyes shone damply. "All we need is a safe place to stay until the baby comes. Then we'll be out of your hair forever."

"Do you have a permit from the Demos?"

Just for a split second, the briefest of flashes, James's gaze strayed toward the woman sitting in the far corner. Short blonde bob, flecked with gray, the ends tucked behind her ears. She didn't acknowledge it, didn't so much as change her expression, but it was enough for me to pick up on the tiny signs – the barely perceptible elevation of breathing rate, the scent of catecholamines, the exchange of fear-pheromones like data packets. Now I knew who was calling the shots. "No," James said, dragging his regard back to me. "She didn't need that before. She came from one of the free communes."

"The father?"

"He died on the barricades," James said. Then, lowering his voice, "That's what she told us, anyway. I don't think she's sure herself."

I let out a slow breath, mulling this over. Asocials. That made things more difficult. An unlicensed pregnancy meant the girl would be blacklisted by the corporations, along with everyone who helped her. James knew that as well as I did: the terrified, desperate look in his eyes told me as much. "It would only be for a short while," he said, but weaker this time, as if he'd already lost hope.

For a moment neither of us said anything. I didn't need enhancements to know that the girl was far too emaciated for someone who is pregnant. The road was no place for the weak and vulnerable. But neither was the Freehold. We had mouths of our own to feed and care for. Children of our own. None of them biologically mine, but that didn't make me love them any less fiercely. "Rest now," I finally said, searching their faces for a sign, a clue, and finding nothing. "We'll talk again."

As James thanked me, I kept my gaze on the woman in the corner, but her head was bowed in wordless gratitude, her features unreadable. They stayed that way as the door closed.

Dusk was falling when I knocked on the door of a wooden prefab at the edge of the housing commune. Landis let me in, still in his farming clothes, black dirt under his nails. "Did anyone see you come here?" he said, with a quick glance through the window.

I shook my head. "All the drones are out for the mapping. I was careful. Doubled back through the cornfield."

He didn't offer me a seat and remained standing himself. The pale wrinkles in his sunburnt face seemed to have gotten deeper. He was only four months into his six-month rotation as Chair, but this was the biggest decision our coop had had to face in a while, perhaps ever.

"It's bad," he said. "People are taking sides. Anderson won't budge on kicking the fugitives out, and some of our freeholders respect that. A crisis doesn't leave room for nuance.

But those who disagree are digging in their heels too. We can't allow a rift in the community."

"What do you think?" I asked.

He shrugged, looked up at the ceiling, as if hoping for a revelation. "As Chair, I can't take sides. But Anderson has a point. Even though it may not be the one he's trying to make."

"The fugitives could be corporate plants." I finished the thought for him. Underhand corporate tactics are something of a specialty of mine. There were plenty of desperate people moving along the coast, ready to do anything for a little food, for a temporary roof over their heads. "One of the megacorps may have sent them here. Just to see what we'll do."

"Right. If we help them, we seal our fate. We may already have done so."

"If we don't," I said, "we split the community."

A heavy feeling came over me, a sense that some indefinable turning point had been reached. If we weren't careful, we could be risking everything we'd worked so hard to build here. Our green valley, our haven from the ugliness of the outside world, would never recover from a blow like that.

Landis knew this too. I could tell from his expression, inscrutable to others, an open book to me. "Whatever you intend to do," he said, walking me to the door, "make sure you do it soon."

In the still evening air, we could hear the tolling of the bell, calling us to supper.

I found the blonde woman washing clothes in a tub behind the shed. A rare moment of isolation: some of her group were inside, others away for their medical checkups.

"You've come a long way," I said.

She started at the sound of my voice. The look she wore was the look of all fugitives anywhere, at once apologetic and fearful. Still, I had the impression my arrival wasn't as much of a surprise as she wanted me to believe.

"Didn't hear you approach." Her voice was warm and pleasant, as was her gaze. Her sleeves were rolled up to her elbows, and her arms were slender arms, but knotty with sinew, the hands narrow but muscular. She held up a wrung-out garment with a wry smile. "When you've got little ones with you, the washing never ends."

I nodded, tipped my head toward the shed. "Have you and your folks been provided for?"

"More than well. Thank you." If the woman was confused by my addressing her instead of James, she gave no sign. "We were almost at the end of our strength when we came here. Especially the children. It's been a long journey."

"Good thing you found us."

"A miracle." She brushed a loose strand of hair from her eyes. In the daylight, she wasn't as old as I'd taken her to be at first. Late thirties, maybe early forties, a little younger than myself. Lean, but not scrawny, her gaze alert, her movements precise and efficient. Something about her demeanor didn't fit in with the others, and that made me uncomfortable. Then again, I'm hardly one to talk.

Wiping one hand on the hem of her shirt, she extended it to me. "Ellen," she said.

I introduced myself, held her hand just a touch longer than was conventionally necessary. Watched her face for a reaction and found none. "I can't imagine," I said, "Walking all that way. The things you must have experienced." Sympathetic expressions don't come naturally to me, but I've had plenty of practice.

"It was hell," she said. "But we survived. Now we have faith that we'll make it."

"Make it up north."

"Over the border." Ellen nodded. "James has some contacts in the Commonwealth. He thinks he can get me a berth on a Pan-Pacific factory ship. Fake papers for the others to get them on the welfare program. Just until they're back on their feet. There's still hope over there." My face must have reflected my thoughts, because her eyes were suddenly sharp. "Is something the matter?"

"How long has your group been on the road?" I stalled, trying to work out a way to break the news gently.

"About a year." Her face wavered in the sunlight. "If there's something I should know, please tell me."

"There is no border anymore." Sometimes it's better to rip off the band-aid in one quick, cruel swipe. "No government, either. Once you get past drug cartel territory around Medford, it's all free trade zones, run by the transnationals. If you're not a registered consumer, you'll be turned back."

Ellen tried to keep her composure, but I could tell that the news shook her. Either that, or she was one of the best actresses I'd ever met. "The ports will still be open," she said, almost defiantly. "Pan-Pac ships must still dock there. They'll be taking on workers."

"Shouldn't be a problem for you, either way." I pointed at the faint silver lines inching out from under her rolled-up sleeve. Corporate barcodes are quite distinct, even deactivated ones.

She said nothing, just pulled down her sleeve slowly. Scratched at the tattoo through the shirt's heavy flannel. "I left that part behind me. It burned with the city and everything else I had."

Smiling, I leaned forward, turning my cheek to give her a better look. In spite of my efforts to remove them, and without facial hair to hide them, my own barcodes are still visible, if one knows what they're looking at. She did.

"They're only skin deep," I said, and that broke the ice between us. Her smile reflected my own. "It's good to have you here, Ellen. You and your people."

"Good to be here." She tossed her hair back self-consciously and seemed uncertain how to proceed. "So, are you in charge here? Or do you speak for the rest?"

I shook my head. "A man named Landis is the cooperative Chair. But we rotate that role every six months and put every decision up for open debate. There are no hierarchies here."

"Sounds complicated."

"It's what we've found to work best." We had each other's measure now. At least I thought so. "How long do you plan on staying here?"

"As long as you'll let us." Ellen leaned with one foot against the wall of the shed. "We can work. All five of us. Even the kids, if you want them to. We'll earn our keep."

"That's not as easy as it sounds."

To her credit, she didn't try to play the guilt card. Either she knew how difficult it would be for us, or had been expecting it, and had a different ace up her sleeve. "I get it. In your shoes, I'd probably do the same thing. You fed and clothed us, and gave us shelter for the night. We can't ask you to do more than that."

I glanced over her head, past the rolling fields, to where Two-Hearts and Paxton were reprogramming the autocombines, the massive engines bellowing in the stillness, then falling silent again, like roars from a pack of distant beasts. "What's it like out there? On the road between the Zones and the farmsteads?"

"Big." Ellen hoisted a basket of washing onto her hip, thought a moment before adding, "Empty. The emptiness gets to you, after a while. You pass by the cities, you see them in the distance, read the road signs. But you know they're off limits to you. Other people are there, breathing, eating, talking. But you'll never be one of them. Makes you feel cut off forever. Like you don't belong to the human race anymore."

"I'm not sure any of us do anymore," I said. "That's probably a good thing."

Her eyes found mine, fixed them. A softening had come into her face, like she was about to laugh, or cry. "It makes you feel like you'd do anything to belong somewhere again. But we can't go back. Even if we had somewhere to go, which we don't. It's not living, what the corporations offer you."

I picked up the other basket, held the shed door open for her. The fugitives inside barely glanced our way, but I wasn't fooled for a moment. I knew they'd been listening.

"They haven't reduced us to that," I said, just to hear the words spoken. "We get to choose. That's the one thing they can't take away from us."

For the briefest of moments, our hands brushed. I let mine linger, and Ellen didn't take hers away. She looked up at me and something seemed to pass between us. More pheromones, perhaps, or simply understanding. "Whatever the cooperative decides, we'll understand. I know it can't be easy for you. But this has to end, one way or another."

By Monday, we had something of a mutiny among the cooperative members, and even the stoic Landis was showing signs of strain.

In their efforts to reprogram the harvesters, Two-Hearts and Paxton had blown the circuit boards. No one could figure out how it happened. The machines squatted in the open like the remains of a dead civilization, surrounded by green waves of bioengineered sorghum. New parts would take days to arrive. Living far from urban sprawl has its advantages, but same-hour delivery is not one of them.

Frightened by the possibility of our big harvest rotting in the fields, Landis had called all hands-on-deck. But the second shift of Freeholders that turned up refused to take their tools. They sat in a silent circle amid the stalks, unmoving, defiant.

"Makes no sense for the newcomers to sit idle," Dawn Mother said, appointing herself speaker, "while we work ourselves into the ground."

"I'll tell you what makes no sense." Anderson, dirt-blackened arms crossed on his chest, refused to budge. "Letting potential saboteurs into our fields. Better to leave this crop to rot right where it came from." The workers of the first shift stood in grim silence behind him, faces set in hard lines.

Eventually, Landis had managed to coax the Freeholders into working, but the blow had been struck, and this was only the first hint of trouble. The next day a group of members confronted Fairchild, who had been sent to order the fugitives back into lockdown. There was no violence, just a lot of shouting and heated words. For their part, the fugitives never complained. They kept to themselves and expressed nothing but gratitude for everything they received.

"We have corn planting coming up next," Landis told me, sounding like he was at the end of his rope. He had called off two cooperative assemblies, afraid to put the fugitive question to the vote, afraid of deepening the rift. But he would have to, and soon.

I spent those days in the systems room, scrounging through pirate data channels for some detail that would unlock the mystery of the fugitives. Wherever I went, I hit a dead end.

All major credit databases returned error reports: none of the names were registered anywhere. It was as if none of them had left any data footprint before showing up here, which couldn't be true. No single corporation had the kind of clout required to completely erase five adults from existence. It was possible that the two kids and the pregnant girl were too young to have made it into a registry. Maybe they'd lived entirely off-grid, born in a cult commune, perhaps, or in one of the militia compounds scattered along the coastline. But that still left four human-sized holes in credit history to be accounted for, The absence of an information trail bothered me more than discovering a false identity, or a corporate blacklist tag.

By the end of the week, Landis was forced to capitulate. The four adult fugitives joined us for the harvesting. Working my shift in the field, my back and knees throbbing like rotten teeth, sweat dripping in my eyes, I would often catch glimpses of Ellen kneeling a few rows down from me. Hidden beneath a wide-brimmed straw hat, she worked quickly and efficiently, more than pulling her weight. Deeply attuned to her presence, I studied her for the smallest tell – an unguarded expression, a signal exchanged with someone else in her group, anything. Ours was a cat-and-mouse game, but I was no longer sure who was the predator and who was prey.

We continued to meet in the evenings, over tea. In out-of-the-way places, without making it look like we were hiding. Talking a lot about nothing of consequence, only rarely giving away pieces of our former lives like precious gems. Ellen was sharp and knowledgeable, the first person in a long time I could talk to intimately.

"Tell me about your time with the corporates," I said, one soft evening filled with the chirring of insects. "Where were you based out of? Bay Area? Organoid City?"

She smiled into her cup, closing her eyes as she inhaled the fragrance of the tea. "Close enough. Went east after the earthquake. The outfit I worked for had privatized the Air Force Reserve. They were blowing up illegal dams on the Colorado. Burning the warlords out of their bunkers."

I whistled in appreciation. "Not bad work, if you can get it."

"It was," Ellen said. "For a while. Then the Water Wars ended, and no one needed a tactician anymore. Things went south quickly after that."

I leaned forward to refill her cup. "We've all made decisions we would rather forget."

"It's all behind me now," Ellen said. "No good can come of stirring up the past."

It was evident that she had been through some terrible ordeal, but she never brought it up, and I knew better than to ask. There are always parts of ourselves that we refuse to share, dark rooms whose doors will forever remain locked.

Slowly but inexorably, the tables were turning, stances hardening. Sometimes I sensed a cold hostility around the supper table, an invisible wall going up between me and part of the Freeholders, as if to shield the fugitives from me. That bothered me too, as much as the missing credit scores did. Because I'd already made up my mind. It was simply a matter of going through with it.

I found Ellen near the hothouses. The year's second tomato harvest had come in like drops of bright red blood under the thermal glass, and a group of Freeholders were sweating in the unseasonable heat, busy with the picking. They pretended not to eavesdrop as I sidled in next to her, asked her if I could have a word.

She was moving slowly, breathing rapidly, her usual energy evaporated like dew from a leaf. The sheen of sweat on her pale face had to do with more than just the temperature. "Just a little touch of something," she said, trying to smile. "I've gotten over worse." But when she took my arm, her touch was clammy, and she leaned on me more heavily than I expected.

I slowed down my pace to match hers, staying out of earshot, but within sight. Dawn Mother had told me that tongues were already wagging: evening rendezvouses, a little autumn romance brewing under the harvest skies. *It's good for you. Makes you seem more human to the others.* I didn't bother correcting her. What Ellen and I had defied categorization, could not be translated into the messy, hormonal interactions of the non-modified. I wasn't sure how to interpret it myself.

By the time we made it to the boundary fence, romance was the furthest thing from Ellen's mind. She put on a game face, but I could hear her breath rattle in her lungs, and she coughed hard enough to retch.

"Should have stayed in bed," she said, apologetic. Yet I could see the banked fire in her gaze, the way it darted from me to the hothouse crew. Wary, calculating.

"It doesn't matter now," I said, helping her sit down on a pile of overturned crates. Reached out and smoothed her hair behind her ear. An innocent gesture: sexual desire was another victim of my modifications I've put myself through, and the one I have the fewest regrets about. But it would look natural to anyone watching. It would look *human*. "It will be over soon. Just rest now."

I saw my words sink in. Hatred flared in her eyes, then panic, then hard resignation. We're all different, but we all cycle through the same emotional patterns at the end. Instinct refuses to accept death: the lungs inflate for one more breath, the heart struggles for another beat.

"How?"

"It's a mycotoxin." I did my best to look just as apologetic as she had moments ago. "Fast-acting and weaponized. Two drops in your tea. It works on your central nervous system."

"No." A pause as she gasped for breath. "Not that. How did you know? What gave us away?"

"Small things." I rubbed her shoulder through her sweat-soaked blouse. There was nothing I could do to reverse it, but I'd make sure she didn't suffer once things got bad. Which they would soon. "Like your barcode. There's no credit profile to go with it. No way to access your employment record. But I know who profited from the Water Wars." Titan, NovAgro, Singenix, Bayer-Monsanto. I didn't recite the names of the megacorps for her: it would have felt disrespectful. "Nothing definitive. More of a precaution, until you just confirmed it."

"There I was, thinking it was my irresistible charm." Something like a smile fought to surface through the spasming muscles of her face. "But you had to have been exposed too."

"Resistant to my own poison," I said. My altered cells produce several strains of toxic metabolites, loaded onto a really nasty viral vector that mutates to match the target's immune system. Antidotes are also in my arsenal, but there was no point telling Ellen that. There were once many like me, designed to be the last line of defense in biotech warfare. The most insidious weapons in the most lethal war never fought and thank whatever gods may be for that. "Outbreaks are impossible to control. Before you know it, the virus has coated itself in proteins, snuck past your defenses, and is wreaking havoc on your system. Killing its host. That's why you were sent here, weren't you? The others may have believed they were escaping, but you knew the truth all along."

Gathering her strength, Ellen pushed herself up to a standing position. "You're too late. We've already done it. Guilty of harboring non-contributors. Asocials. When the conglomerates find out—"

The rest of it was wiped out by another bout of coughing. One of the women poked her head out of the hothouse, asked Ellen if she was all right. Trembling with effort, Ellen smiled, waved her away.

"They won't do anything," I said. "Not after word gets out about you. Botched crop sabotage attempt. Dead body carrying traces of mycotoxin. There may be no government agency regulating food security, but the megacorps take such threats seriously. It'll be in their interest to keep us quiet, or they'll be blamed. They'll lay off us, at least for a good long while."

When I offered my arm, she took it, and we walked along the fence wall. Warm sun on our faces, the smell of flowers and freshly turned soil. It's our own slice of heaven, far from the rising oceans, from the barren plains, from the fear and want of the cities. No wonder others want to take it from us. No wonder we fight so hard to keep it. Even after we've turned the world into a barren, near-uninhabitable hell, we still hold onto the hope of paradise in our hearts. We have to. Otherwise, all this, our existence on this dying planet, would be meaningless.

I spoke up before she had managed to phrase her question. "We won't kill the others. We're not monsters. But they have to go."

Ellen shrugged. "They knew what they signed up for. Did they have a choice?"

"Did any of us?" she asked, a blush of anger suffusing her sallow cheeks. But it was short-lived, her cardiovascular system shutting down all unnecessary circulation, trying to spare its failing pump. "No one's innocent. Even the kids are indentured. There's no other way to survive. Disease, superstorms, droughts, famines. Cycle after cycle, while the corporations feed on the ashes."

"Who sent you?"

The name she gave me meant nothing to me, but I filed it for future reference. We were past deception now. The pain would only get worse, and I had the control switch. "Is it an agro conglomerate?" I asked. "You don't owe them anything anymore. Unburden yourself. Tell me where they are."

"Everywhere. Every moment." A low moan escaped her and she doubled over, clinging to me for support. When she raised her eyes, they shone with malice. "Do you think you can be safe here? In your own little fortress, while the rest of the world dies? They want you under their heel." She was breathing hard, sipping air in small gasps. "Before the idea spreads. Before other places follow your example. This is one of the last chunks of fertile soil on the entire continent. You're a splinter in their eye. They won't stop until they've pried you out. Every last freeholder."

She wasn't telling me anything I didn't already know. "Maybe," I said. "But this is my only chance to reclaim a life worth living. It may crash and burn in the end, but I have to try. I couldn't live with myself if I didn't."

"We all tell ourselves the same story," she said. "That we can make things better. Find our way back to what we used to be. But we can't."

"Was it really worth this, Ellen? Whatever they offered you?"

The wheezing sound she made had to be a laugh. "No, it wasn't," she said, threading her arm through mine, pulling me closer, like the lover I could never be. "But then, what ever is?"

As I leaned closer, the merciful lethal dose under my tongue, I felt her breath leaving her body, fluttering against my lips like a trapped bird.

The next day Landis and I stood at the eastern gate, waiting for a NovAgro mobile unit to pick up Ellen's body. We were sweating inside our hazmat suits, partly with anxiety, partly because of the stifling heat. An unnecessary, uncomfortable precaution – the mycotoxin was a tailored assassin version, not a contamination strain – but one that would lend support to my version of the story. A bioterrorist had snuck in to infect our crops: something had gone wrong, and she'd ended up killing herself by mistake. There would be no autopsy, because the conglomerates would rush to bury the evidence.

There would be a wave of testing and independent commissions, followed by recriminations, each conglomerate suspecting its rivals of targeting the freehold by mistake. Paranoia and conspiracies ruled the world beyond our doorstep. That was their problem now.

Earlier that morning, the remaining fugitives had been escorted to the gate. With Ellen gone, the rest had caved under questioning. Told us everything they knew, which wasn't much. Even if they didn't believe the sabotage explanation, they knew better than to kick up a fuss. The cold hard looks on faces that only yesterday had seemed so friendly made certain of that. Freeholders live and die by the harvest, and this threat united us like never before.

"What happens after this?" Landis asked after the sealed coffin had been loaded into the refrigerated unit, suited and masked techs handling it with the delicacy usually reserved for explosive devices. "Because whoever sent this lot will be back. It's just a matter of time."

I turned toward him. Impossible to see his eyes through the visor, but I focused on where I thought they would be. This was not a time for platitudes. Rains would come, and rains would fail; drought and pestilence would decimate our fields. But the freehold would endure. That certainty came to me as I gazed out past the gate, where the vehicle carrying Ellen's body was disappearing in a plume of dust.

"We watch," I said. "We wait. When they come, we'll be ready."

Because I'm a weapon, designed to pass unnoticed. To infiltrate brightly lit corporate arcologies, and let the poison in my blood, in my glands, spread its terrible gospel. Next time we would strike first.

The corporations had killed the outside world, but we would protect our green garden of plenty. Fight for it to the last Freeholder. Because only kin mattered, and sweat and toil had made a bond stronger than blood.

Our war, our long, silent war, was only beginning.

LINE OF DUTY

A peeling green metal door is set in the graffiti-covered pre-fab wall, one in a dreary row of identical structures. The windows are gone, boarded, and painted over. Dim alleys lead off the street with dimmer shapes moving inside them.

I walked five blocks from the drop-off point to get here, and it's the same reek of piss and shit and desperation everywhere. We're forty-five minutes from downtown, but the scene could just as easily be Rabat, or Tobruk, or any war-torn, blighted slum along the Mediterranean coast. There we fought door-to-door, street-to-street, never knowing who to trust, which direction the next danger would come from. Viral agents and smart mines on one side, religious militias on the other, stoned out of their minds and often mixing up enemies and allies. Hard to compete with chemically induced visions of the Gardens of Paradise, rivers of milk and honey and wine guaranteed, or your money back.

Here in the grim bowels of the city, there are no houris. There are also no utility conglomerates, and the muted light of the biolumes don't reach far into the shadowed corners. But there are eyes down here that watch from the darkness, eager and hungry. Fourteen years in IP enforcement and two tours in the Maghreb during the biotech wars – the ones that officially never happened – have taught me as much.

I adjust my arm in the stiff, uncomfortable sling as I limp toward the door, doing my best to blend in. If the tip-off was right, and this place is more than just a junkie shooting gallery, my arrival will already have been noticed. Plenty of spots to install a microcamera, or stand watch in the shadows, keeping an eye on the foot traffic. Even if I haven't been made yet, these warrens are full of dangers, and a crippled, lone man makes for an attractive target.

My knock is answered by a woman. She's about my age but looks younger with clear skin and a well-fed, conditioned body. She belongs here even less than I do. Her wary eyes take me in, but she's silent, waiting for me to speak first.

I smile weakly through the cuts and bruises on my face, make a show of raising my cradled arm an inch or two. There is no immediate reaction. When the woman opens her mouth, her voice is as flat and indifferent as her eyes.

"What do you want?"

My wetware scans her face. Biodata pops up in the circle of the recognition display, name and date of birth and address, corporate affiliation, credit rating. That last number is significantly higher than my own. It still amazes me that there are people who do this, risk everything for the dirty, starving dregs of humanity who inhabit this underworld. But I don't let my amazement show. "I heard you can help me," I say, keeping my voice down to a mumble. It makes me feel as pathetic as I look. "Just a scan and a platelet shot. Please."

"We don't do that sort of thing here," she says. "I don't know where you think you are, or who sent you. But this is not the place. There's a self-med up by the train station, near the square. You can try your luck there."

"I know what you're thinking," I say. "But I'm not like the others down here. I had a job on the factory floor. That's how I got hurt. They took away my bennies after it happened. If I take care of this right away, I could still get my job back."

The woman makes a face like she's heard it all before. Dregs and junkies are incredibly creative when it comes to shifting blame for their own problems. "Get the hell out of here before I call the patrol," she says, not budging from the door." Gonzales buzzes in my cochlear implant, angry as a wasp, telling me to stay on script. I ignore him. Our team analyzed footage from cameras and facial scanners, traced the prescription and pickup patterns, and checked out the anonymous hotline reports. Enough for a reasonable suspicion. But no amount of number crunching can replace my gut feeling, the extra sense I've developed over the years, and it's telling me I'm in the right place.

Behind the woman, behind that door, is an illegal clinic, and I'm getting inside, one way or another.

I lower my voice further feeling the subvocal modulators kicking in. Not exactly company-approved, but Compliance is happy to turn a blind eye for an enforcer with my collection rate.

"I understand how risky this is for you," I say to the woman, moving closer to block off her view of the street, in case someone in my backup jumps the gun. "But my sister and her kid, they're on my credit right now. My wife and I are waiting for our child permit from the Demos. This couldn't have happened at a worse time." My tear ducts well up, reacting to the thrum of my voice – a preprogrammed reaction to enhance emotional appeal. "If I can't get back on the floor, all four of us will be out on the street. Please. At least some painkillers. I've got nowhere else to go."

She says nothing, but I feel a small pang of triumph. The line about kids gets them every time. She slams the door shut, then opens it again, and lets me into the murky corridor beyond, almost dragging me in. Her grip is strong and sure.

"Wait here," she tells me before walking down the passage, through an open door. Blue light flickers inside, the way old screens do when they start to break down with images bleeding into one another. I switch my implants to transmission mode and shuffle forward, taking in the layout of the doors and rooms, the angles and corners, peering into the room the woman just entered.

Jackpot.

There's a stockpile of equipment here, much of it outdated, but in good condition. Bioscanners, sterilizers, medical kits, even what looks like a basic-model autosurgeon, sharp arms gleaming in the corner. Cabinets full of every drug imaginable. Enough contraband to stock a chain of self-med centers: they must have been accumulating it for years. I play dumb, but my pulse picks up, my irises open, adrenaline flooding my system, sharpening my senses. Whatever this is, it goes deeper than our Intel ever estimated.

"Stay there," says the woman, meaning I'm not to go into the room. She's reaching into a locker, rummaging, pulling out a container of red-and-yellow vials. I zoom in as the logo and serial number flash under her hand. Two others are in the room with her, both men, both middle-aged and running to fat. Clearly in the right place, at the wrong time.

I wait a few beats, listening as Gonzales and the strike team maneuver into position outside the door. Then I follow the woman into the room with a clueless expression – a dumb, ignorant yokel awestruck by his surroundings. One of her companions lowers his dataglasses to glare at me. "Hey," he says, blinking past the display on his lenses. "Hey. You can't come in here."

My neuromesh scans their postures, their expressions, the space around them. Prediction software fills my view with probability scenarios. I raise my arms. "Just looking," I say, taking another step forward. "Quite the collection you got here. Did it fall off the back of a truck, or something?"

The man gapes at me for a second, then pushes out his chest and moves to block my way. "Out," he says, mouth twitching. "Or we'll have you removed. What happens here is none of your business."

"Beg to differ." I let that hang in the air for a moment. "You're very much my business. All of you."

The woman jerks round, dropping the vials. Glass shatters on the dirty linoleum. She starts to scold me for my trespass; then her eyes widen, the indifference on her face melts away. Underneath is a complex brew of emotions – anger, and hate, and undiluted fear. She knows why I'm really here and she knows there's no salvation for her.

It's the second man whose reaction takes me by surprise. In a smooth, practiced motion he drops the tablet he's holding and rolls to the floor, his hand reaching for the small of his back. *Security training*, I have time to think, and then my matrix takes over, a whirl of neurochemicals and programmed movements, reality retreating behind a smeary screen.

The ReactiSense of the holster concealed in my sling whips the pistol into my hand a split second before my brain can send the right signal to the right nerve. A difference too negligible to measure with a clock, but enough to close the gap between life and death. Before my biological senses are aware of it, my eleven-millimeter SIG Sauer has already fired, an electrochemical flash accelerating six caseless slugs toward the man on the floor.

He's got the drop on me, but the matrix adjusts an order of magnitude faster than the human brain. Large-caliber bullets punch through him in a pink mist, painting the wall behind him. He's dead before his arm brings round the useless weapon. I don't even bother sidestepping his unaimed shot as I walk through the doorway.

Frozen in front of me, the first man dies before he's fully understood what's happened. My SIG Sauer blasts the top of his head clean off above the nose. Red matter slaps wetly on the flatscreen behind him, oozes down over blinking vitals icons. Back in the corridor, the door explodes, Gonzales and Miller rushing into the building, followed by others. The silent pad of SlipGrip tacboots on the floor, shouts and harsh orders, blasts of gunfire.

The woman's stunned gaze moves from me to the nearest console. Shock has kept her paralyzed through those few seconds of violence, but I know what she's thinking now. "Don't," I say quietly, leveling the pistol at her center of mass.

There aren't many rules in my line of work. Track down and eliminate illegal clinics. Seize the goods. Limited violence is a distant third directive and open to interpretation. Protecting ourselves is important, but the asocials are rarely armed or trained in firearms. The menace they present to society as a whole, the damage they do to our way of life, is far greater than physical. Without a system, without order, no one survives.

The main trouble is that these people see themselves as *heroes*. Rules don't apply to heroes, which makes them unpredictable. Rather than try to save herself, all she can think of is the hidden kill switch, and there's nothing heroic about that. Just another pathetic, asocial scab, trying to strike a blow against the world.

Miller and Gonzales and the rest of the team are in the corridor behind me. The mop-up operation is complete. But it feels like the woman and I are alone in the building, alone in the world. Our eyes meet and I read her intention in them even before she goes for the console.

I pull the trigger and lose myself in the suppressed boom.

Miller and I soar up the causeway in the armored cruiser, the city's spires thrusting up beneath our wheels, gilded with afternoon gold. After the grime and despair of the undercity, its gravelike darkness, the sun feels like a blessing on my skin.

My partner doesn't look blessed. Pale and wan, he hunches in the passenger seat and avoids eye contact. We've raided asocial-run clinics before, but this is the first time he's witnessed the shock and awe our cutting-edge weapons and enhancements can inflict. I know what's eating at him, and I wish I could say that the bloody work we've signed up for gets better with time. It doesn't. But it gets easier, that's for sure. To break the silence and give him the opening he needs, I say, "Good job back there. Management appreciates initiative. I'll put you in for a spot bonus."

Miller says nothing, only nods his head absently. "What was the final tally?"

His response is a long time coming, the words spat out as if they'd been choking him. "Twenty-four. Not counting the three in the front office. The ones you—"

"Liquidated," I say, when I see that he won't. "Recycled their credit points back into the system."

The words trigger some sort of flashback: my face sweating under a gas mask as I descend into a bunker. Bodies lie slumped against the walls, in chairs, in beds. Untouched, but sweating blood. Modern warfare at its best – a hemorrhagic fever agent pumped into the air ducts.

We drive in silence for a minute. It's still daylight, but the sea of corporate logos already shimmers and shifts all around us, ads beckoning, promising, seducing. Before I know it, I've racked up a shopping list in my dataglasses.

"Liquidated." Miller repeats the word reflectively. "Is that what happens to them? To all of them?"

"It's not supposed to. The asocials we arrest, the ones running the clinics, are released if they don't present an immediate danger. But they can't go back into the credit system. Some are admitted to labor camps. Some sent to coastal reclamation projects or salvage work in the Zones."

He mulls this over for a moment. "The people in those rooms," he says, swallowing hard. He almost says *patients*, then remembers his orientation and catches himself in time. "The ones getting treatment. I don't think they'll be volunteering for any labor camps. Half of them were practically dead. The rest could barely get out of bed."

"They get the needle," I say. "Then the composter. It's humane. They don't feel a thing."

Miller exhales and runs a hand through his hair.

"I know it feels wrong," I say. An annoying icon pops into my vision: I dismiss it with the flick of a finger. "But it's the only way that makes sense. Society can't go back to the old days. That's how we ended up in this shit to begin with."

"I don't need an ethics lesson, Haldane."

My own throat tightens, but with anger. "Yeah, I think you do. Because you don't know how it was before."

Truth be told, I don't either. The only memories I have are of my terrified parents pushing me through crowds of panicked people, of uniformed government soldiers handing out food in ready-heat packages, of barbed-wire barricades going up, then walls, blotting out the blighted parts of the city. But I'm on a roll and making a point.

"You don't know what it was like being a slave to other people's wants and needs. Sacrificing ourselves for the worthless and the irresponsible. It was chaos. The whole city was one big containment zone. All because the politicians went soft on the freeloaders. Even as the world burned."

Chastened, my partner sinks into his seat. "It just seems a little extreme, you know? I'm okay with shutting down the clinics. Arresting criminals and smugglers. But these people, these asocials, they're not stealing from the Company. They're buying the stuff on their own dime. Isn't that in line with exercising their consumer rights?"

Brainwashed, I realize, with a shock of dismay, making a mental note to check Miller's background file for red flags. "All those drugs, all that equipment, could have been sold to real people. Good, solid citizens-consumers who work hard to qualify for their credit. Instead, they were wasted on the freeloading poor, who are going to die anyway. Forgive me for not seeing any sense in that."

But something he said has turned off a light in my head. For a moment, I'm back at the illegal clinic, the memory is so vivid I can smell the piss and disinfectant and fear. Something about the vials and the numbers, the woman's hand on the drug cabinet. Yet I can't remember what it is.

As I chase down this elusive clue, I lose track of my thoughts. My tirade suddenly feels pointless. Fortunately, Miller has seen sense: I can tell by the subtle relaxation of his shoulders and his breathing pattern. He accepts my explanation because he *wants* to believe it. So, I believe it too.

Two days later, another report of a clinic comes in. A red icon blinks in my lens, interrupting my digging through paperwork. Gonzales himself has forwarded me the address, which means it must be big.

I take the elevator to the sub-basement garage and get into the cruiser. Miller's not there yet, so I take a few minutes scrolling through the onboard computer, changing search parameters and permutations, still not entirely sure what I'm looking for, or what I'm going to find there.

What I do know is that things are not adding up. According to the records, all the drugs we seized in the raid have been destroyed. The weights logged in by the incinerator facility reconcile with those shipped out by our dispatch bot. But in the file the drugs are marked as knockoffs, dangerous counterfeits, which isn't what I saw at the clinic. Gonzales signed off on the report himself.

I'm so absorbed I barely notice my partner fling the door open and slide into the passenger seat. Clumsily, I try to hide what I'm doing, only succeeding in making it more obvious. Fortunately, Miller is too distracted to notice. "Just got off the phone with P&A," he says, giving me a pointed look of reprimand. "They had a bunch of questions about the stuff we requested. Something about serial numbers on the drugs we seized in the raid. I told them I'd get back to them." He pauses a beat. "So. You want to tell me what that was all about?"

"I asked for some reports," I say, hoping that my tone discourages further discussion. Going over the head of Gonzales, the shift supervisor, to ask for the reports is not good protocol. If I'm found out, I could be in minor trouble and major trouble if my hunch is right. There's no point involving my partner. Not yet, anyway.

Miller is smart enough to leave it at that. The heavy cruiser guns to life and we roll out of the garage, up the winding ramp to the connector. Within minutes, we're barreling out of the arcology's industrial park enroute to the place we're supposed to check out Sunlight forms an arc over the causeway as we plunge into the concrete and glass of downtown. The cruiser's autonav takes over, slides the vehicle smoothly into the rush of inbound traffic. In the distance, the ugly gray of the zone wall rises like a bad omen.

My partner's face falls as he leans over the navscreen and sees our destination. "You've got to be shitting me," he says.

"Containment Area Southwest. Hope all your shots are up to date." A suspicion has crept into my head, sly and slick like a leech, battening onto my thoughts. Someone's diverting drugs and equipment from the evidence locker. With a little more digging, I could figure out who exactly, but lately it's hard for me to focus. They nag at me, all the things Miller said on the ride home, after that last raid, and all the things he didn't say. They won't be put out of my mind.

"We're not supposed to go over the wall." Miller groans and sinks back into the headrest. "We have no jurisdiction there."

"Nope." Already the traffic is getting thicker, vehicles slowing down, joining the miles-long tail for the checkpoint. I feel the brakes kick in, consider hitting the siren, then decide against it. If we're heading out to the Zones, the last thing we want to do is draw attention to ourselves. "But it's part of the job, kid. We'll make a stop after that. Follow up on this hunch I have. You okay with that?"

I don't want to share my hunch with Miller. If I'm wrong, he'll still be able to claim deniability. No use sticking both our necks out, at least not yet.

"I don't like it," Miller says.

"We drive by, we check it out," I say, trying to sound more casual than I feel. "If we see anything, we call for backup. If we don't, we head back. You can say you thought it had been greenlit. I'm the senior partner. I'll take the blame."

Popping a couple of neurostim tabs, I hold the bottle out to Miller, who shakes his head. He's into organic coffee from the Parana States, weird herbal blends from the Rim. "That shit is poison. Gives me headaches."

"But it gets you nice and sharp," I say, chewing the tabs to make them work faster. The doctors don't agree. They say that all I'm doing is damaging my teeth. But nice teeth look out of place on a corpse.

Miller snaps back something, probably a smart-ass response. I'm not paying attention. In my head, corporate flags snap in the wind from the gray sea. It's quiet – the ominous quiet in the trenches. The rolling golden dunes of the desert spread behind the dead city, sterilized by tactical nukes. Then the scene falls into a hole, a tunnel, as the neurostim kicks in. Everything inside the tunnel moves faster and in sharp focus, the world outside it slowing down, becoming dull.

I let myself go and join the rush.

We park in the middle of suburban ruin.

Abandoned homes and looted strip malls lie under a freeway ramp ravaged by salvage machines. Here are the demons we banished from the civilized parts of the city: poverty, disease, addiction, violent crime. Hopelessness hangs in the dirty air like a pall. Furtive shadows dart between the walls; graffiti call for DEATH TO CORPORATIST FILTH.

The place is neglected, but not deserted. My augments pick up rusty rainwater collectors, power lines stretched like tightropes between the roofs. Vermin are impossible to exterminate.

The torn-up ramp is too jagged for even the cruiser's armored tires to negotiate. We step out of the car and survey the desolation below. I unclip my holster but leave the SIG Sauer in it. Our facial barcodes already mark us as outsiders and obvious targets. Avoiding each other's firing lines, we walk down the baking concrete toward the blighted houses.

In Orientation, they teach you how to read space and its components and take into consideration angles and geometries. There are tranks to calm you down, stims to help you focus, and crank to speed up reaction time, but some things can't be taught or inhaled or dermed or implanted. Some instincts you develop the good old-fashioned way: through natural selection. Right now that ineffable sense is screaming in my head, drowning out the matrix and the 'ware, recognizing the space we're descending into for what it is: a killing field.

Miller doesn't have the same background, but he can feel the wrongness in the air. He points to the ugly brick cube to our left, the remains of a commercial unit. The positioning icon hovers directly over it. Torched skeletons of cars, the old gasoline models, line the street, picked clean like bones. Blackened houses stretch in all directions. "That doesn't look right," he says, hand hovering near his holster.

"You don't say." I double-check the coordinates in my 'glass. There's no mistake. Weeds sprout through cracks in the sidewalk. Once we leave the ramp's concrete pillars, there's a whole lot of open space between us and the door. It's an odd place for an illegal clinic.

I tap into my subvocals, trying to raise Rapid Response to get us some backup. Nothing. Maybe the signal doesn't reach this far. Maybe the comm systems are down. Too many maybes for my taste.

The unease in my gut merges with the neurostim, a white-hot comet spinning fiery circles inside my skull. This stuff gets you nice and tight and alert, but tends to make you a little impulsive, a little less rational. Great for when a cranked-up paramilitary rushes screaming at you from the trenches of Tobruk or Carthage, virus-bomb strapped to his chest, laughing as you shoot him to pieces. Not so great when you're standing in an empty street, trying to puzzle what's about to happen.

The smart thing would be to head back to the cruiser, drive back to the city, and present our case to senior management. But I already suspect that won't work, because some of them are in on it. Have to be. There's no telling how deep the infiltration has gone.

"Come on," I say to Miller, with enough false confidence for both of us. "We came all this way, might as well take a look."

Closer up, the door is a plywood sheet nailed over a rectangular hole, the windows wear cataracts of DuraPlast sheeting. I scan the facade for genny cables, solar cells, tell-tale signs of a power supply. If this place is hoarding drugs, they need to keep them refrigerated. But I don't see any.

"Dead," Miller says, reaching the same conclusion. I see the tension go out of his shoulders and back. "Probably a false report or a system glitch. Let's ring the doorbell and make sure."

"Stay where you are, Miller." From the edge of my vision, I see the loose corner of a sheet flutter slightly, exposing the darkness within. In that darkness, something is moving.

He turns round, a smartass quip on his lips, and the first shot that punches through the DuraPlast takes him in the neck, a neat round hole as wide as the tip of his little finger, immediately filling with blood. The second bullet blows off his lower jaw, erasing the half-formed expression of surprise. Then all hell breaks loose and I hear slugs thumping everywhere, but I can't see what's happening to Miller. I'm already rolling across the broken asphalt, never mind the scrapes and cuts, into the dubious cover of a burned-down car.

Lying in ambush is harder than the immersion films make it out to be. Sooner or later the body cramps, the face itches, the weapon gets heavy and needs to be braced. My 'ware picked up on one of these minor twitches behind one of the windows, which is why I'm still alive.

A hailstorm of gunfire explodes from the building, rounds pinging off concrete and scarred metal. I'm painfully aware that the ruined hulk offers no protection at all, that a charge-pistol slug can go through inches of thick wall, regardless of the caliber. If I don't move quickly, I'm as dead as my partner. Even if my distress call registered back at the station, I may as well be on Mars as far as help is concerned.

Fear normally paralyzes you and erodes your focus. But the neurostim feeds on it, the matrix latching onto the urge to survive, edging out all else including any rage and guilt I feel over Miller's death. Just like it did in the trenches. Rage won't bring him back. All that's left to do is exact my pound of flesh, rain bloody retribution down on his killers.

Pulling out my pistol, I let my mesh extrapolate the locations of the shooters. Every shot they fire is a vector leading straight to my target, and they're giving me plenty of data to work with. At least three in the windows, one on the roof. They're trying to pin me down to give the guy on top a clear shot.

Deep breath, then I'm rising, springing, with the 'ware taking over, I squeeze the trigger. The accelerator pin hammers down eight times in a second, the matrix correcting between each shot. Intervals too short to measure, but survival is a matter of nanoseconds now.

Plastic sheeting blows in as if from a hurricane, and I hear a muffled scream under the gunfire. Bullets pound the spot I'm no longer standing in. Running toward the building, I pour a torrent of death at a second target. I can't confirm any hits, but the shooting stops for a moment. Sweeping the SIG Sauer left to right, I strafe the windows blindly, and somehow manage to reach the far end of the wall.

The haze in my head clears. I slam a fresh clip into the pistol. My back is pressed up against the prefab siding, my breath coming in short gasps. They know where I am, but they can't see me, not without showing their faces.

I'm hit in several places. My lungs are laboring and my implant grafts are pumping to clear metabolites to keep blood supply going. Warm redness snakes around my left wrist, soaks the bottom of my trousers. There's pain too, a great crashing wave suspended above me, but for the moment it's held in check by the invisible wall of the chemicals.

Voices are coming from inside. I can't make out the words, but I hear the panic. Raising my weapon, I watch the roof for movement. Nothing stirs up there. The street is just as empty as before, except for Miller's body face down in the dust. In death, he looks smaller, shrunken like a popped balloon.

Stalemate for the time being. But I can't count on being left alone, or on backup showing up on time. Plus, it's personal now.

I creep over to the door, pull it open, flinch from the anticipated shots. But there aren't any. Someone is breathing heavily down the dark hallway, air bubbling in punctured lungs. That's what the boys used to sound like in the Tobruk trenches after a lungful of mycotoxin.

I hear footsteps from the inner darkness while trying to stay silent. I slip through the doorway on my right and wait, but they don't come any closer. The only light is coming through the gaping square of the window. Even the walls have been stripped to remove wiring and insulation. A blackened mattress lies in one corner, ancient crank ampoules littering the dirty floor.

This isn't an illegal clinic, but a trap.

One of the shooters slumps against the wall in the corner with shots through the chest and guts and his submachine gun out of reach. Not a crankhead, nor an asocial: as the light shifts, I can see the barcode tattoos on his face and hands. One of us. He makes another bubbling sound and gives me a pleading look.

I think about Miller dead in the street, and for a moment I'm tempted to leave the dying killer right where he is. But ultimately we're no different, he and I, and while there are few formal rules of engagement, it's the unwritten ones we all live and die by. So I flip the pistol to single-fire and put a round through his forehead.

The building is eerily silent. I don't know if this means the bastards have given up, or are merely sitting tight waiting for reinforcements. In the room across the corridor, a glassy-eyed corpse lies on its back sporting a neat row of holes across its chest. This one is a woman, but her codes tell me nothing. I pick up her submachine, the clip still half-charged. I try her comms but get only crackling silence.

Back out in the corridor, I head deeper into the building. My lenses narrows in the low light. A staircase looms in my adjusted vision. The drugs are wearing off and the first pain front is pushing through them. I chew my last neurostim tablet and dry-swallow the chalky residue. Swinging the submachine gun upward, I let loose two controlled volleys up the steps, mindful of the ricochet.

I realize I'm delirious, but my head feels good, like a rotten tooth being pulled out, leaving behind clean pain. Babbling in street Arabic, I point the submachine at a flitting shadow on the upper landing, hold the trigger down until the clip is dead. Switching to the pistol, I climb a few steps to see the roof shooter, mangled beyond recognition. Looks like he wins: he gets to Paradise first.

Someone is shrieking, the sound ringing in the close confines of the stairwell.

Down below, a door slams against the wall. Two dull punches to my ribs, and the taste of metal rises into my throat, but I'm ready, friend, I've been waiting for you.

The SIG Sauer cuts the last shooter in two as he turns to flee. Swiss precision, Rim engineering, NorAm overwhelming force. Momentum sends him tumbling to the floor: on hands and knees, he crawls toward the front door, leaving a dark wet trail behind. My arms and legs aren't working as well as they're supposed to, but my aim is still true.

Yes, sir. As good as it was in Tobruk. Better, in fact. The eye I lost in that shitshow of an evacuation was replaced by a vatgrown organ. Twenty-twenty vision, ten-year warranty and returns free of charge.

I plunge after him in the dark, blood trickling from my smiling lips, wetting my chin.

When the world swims back into focus, I'm on the floor, back against the wall. Shirt and pants stuck to my skin with blood. Mostly my own. The pain is enormous, but it's going away slowly, replaced by a great, invasive cold.

I'm a child of the age of environmental collapse. Winter is as alien a concept to me as the outer reaches of the Solar System. But now winter is coming for me, and I understand why my ancestors feared the dark and cold.

From that darkness, someone is calling my name.

I sit up. It's not a hallucination. I hear it again, followed by the approaching tread of SlipGrip shoes. Drugs must still be circulating through my system, because everything is in sharp focus: I hear each pebble distinctly as it rolls underfoot.

"Haldane." Gonzales's voice, booming through the empty hallway. "What the hell happened here?"

My finger dips into the cooling pool beneath me. Traces patterns inside it. My other hand wraps around the SIG Sauer. "Over here," I say, but only in my head. What actually comes out is a kind of croaking moan.

He appears in a doorway on the far side of the room, wearing body armor, cradling a submachine with a folding stock. What with the darkness and blurring vision, I can't see his eyes. "Any hostiles left?" he says, inching the barrel up.

"Got them all," I say. "Four of them. They had the drop on us, but I made them pay."

Gonzales nods, and I wait for him to lower the weapon. But he doesn't. "Let's get you out of here," he says, then moves his jaw to send a message through his subvocals. "Can you walk?"

I make vague noises but force myself to my knees. Gonzales is in on it. He set me up. There's no rescue team waiting outside, no way out of here for me alive. I wonder why he's still keeping up the charade.

Which means that I'm to blame for Miller. I killed him just as surely as if I'd pulled the trigger. Sorrow stirs up, but I clamp down on it, tuck it behind the icy wall of drugs. I can't bring Miller back, but I can make his killers pay.

"You say they're all dead?"

"Well." I try to brace the pistol from a kneeling position. Slide my finger on the trigger. The walls are still spinning as I take aim. "Not all of them, I suppose."

Reflexes save Gonzales. He doesn't try to turn nor return fire, but instead just throws himself back into the corridor. I can hear him hiss quietly from the darkness.

I crawl across the room to the doorway. Muzzle flashes light up the corridor when I pop my head out, ducking back immediately. Concrete dust grits between my teeth.

"You fuck," Gonzales rages from the dark. "Had to stick your nose where it doesn't belong, did you? Couldn't leave well enough alone."

In truth, I had no idea Gonzales was involved. But he overplayed his hand with the fake tracker and the ambush. Easy enough for a shift supervisor to arrange and easier still to cover up. "What happened, Marco? Got too big for your britches? Couldn't resist making a buck on the side?"

He curses at me, and I wait for another burst of fire, but it doesn't come. "How did you figure it out?"

"Three years in Repo," I say. "Enough to tell nano-stamped drug vials from counterfeits. Enough to figure out someone's putting a small fortune into their own pocket. Maybe the guy with the keys to the evidence locker."

I listen for movement, but there's nothing. Gonzales digesting what he's just heard. Or maybe just too tired to argue.

"So what was this about, really?" I ask. "Padding out your retirement? Or the usual sob story – addiction, gambling, whores? Be honest, now. Neither of us is leaving this place, except feet first."

Then it hits me, his silence speaking louder than anything he might say. "You're one of them," I say. "You're not doing this for money."

"People are dying out here, Haldane." His voice is calmer now. I listen for stealthy movement, imagine him creeping down the corridor. Whose augments will react first? "I don't know how you can close yourself off to it. But it's hell out in the Zones, and it's no better in the incorporated areas. People are stomped on and discarded. Just because some genescrubbed fuck in an expensive suit doesn't like the last quarter's numbers and decides to cut costs. Because human life has no value anymore."

"Freeloaders." I'm too stunned to articulate a more coherent comeback. If they got to Gonzales, how far has the cancer spread? "Dregs. Credit-zeros. You want to save them so they can keep being a drain on society. On real people like you and me."

"That's corporate doublespeak. We're all credit-zeros, man. Deep inside, you know who the real bloodsuckers are. But they control the messaging, convincing us that black is white and white and black. That's how they keep us at each other's throats."

"I trusted you," I say, tightening my grip on the pistol, which suddenly feels very heavy. "I put my life in your hands, you asshole."

Do I try to end it in a rush, or drag it out? Gonzales with nowhere to go and I with nothing to lose.

"I did it for my brother," Gonzales says, barely audible. For a moment, my blood-starved brain gropes for the meaning of his words. Then I get it. He wants to explain his madness. Justify it to himself. "His younger son got sick. It was either the needle or an illegal clinic. I made my choice and never looked back."

"Some choice."

"I'm at peace with God," Gonzales says, and he sounds so close I feel I could reach out and touch him. "At peace with myself. What about you, Haldane? What do you see when you look in the mirror? Or when you close your eyes at night? Does anything matter to you anymore? Did it ever?"

My bars, I want to say. *My ink. My pride in being part of something greater.* In belonging. My individualism, the expression of my free will. But my voice is very small, and I can't quite force it past my lips.

What do I see when I close my eyes? I see the sun on the white walls of the compound in Tobruk. I see the dead – bobbing in dirty water, stranded on barbed wire, bleeding out on the ground.

But I'm not one of the dead. Not yet.

I feel my lips peel back in a bloody grin, my implants pump out one last chemical surge. As I spin through the doorway, pistol blazing, I have the answer to Gonzales's question.

Right or wrong, this is my choice.

BEACHED

The sky leans in above the sharp angles of broken concrete and peers though the casements of empty windows. There is a sullen heat in the air, unrelieved by the breeze gusting in from the ocean whose briny smell only adds to the swamp fumes of the sunken town. Silty water surrounds the building on all sides, still and scummed with oil that shines like a rainbow in the sun, surrounded by the foul, tepid breath of the drowned buildings.

Nasser scuttles across the crumbling edges, hands and feet ferret-quick on the warm cement, a wraith in a group of near-identical wraiths picking through ruins left half-submerged by the hurricane. At the front of the sunbaked terrace, Casemiro stops and raises his arm, and the children crouch down as quiet as mice. Their backs are long and their limbs thin. Their knobby spines push out under sweat-sheened dark skin. Then the group is on the move again, bare feet racing down an incline and onto a flat rooftop terrace, the children careful to keep their heads down behind the parapet. As one, they perk their ears and listen in the hot and humid afternoon. They've grown used to uncertainty and danger over the course of their short lives. Green Armband snipers occupy the neighborhoods to the north, bored and listless in the heat and eager for some moving target practice. Their scopes can scan the roofs like an open book.

Following his friends' cues, Nasser crouches down and slows his breathing, despite the frenetic pulsing of his heart.

Ever since the great storms battered the seafront, his group has descended from Bairro Morro to comb through the remains of the town. There are treasures to be found amid the devastation: small electronics, household items, once an entire room full of reconstituted meals in waterproof packaging. The ruined towers were once highrises, columns of shiny windows behind which handsomely dressed men and women worked in air-conditioned and sun-filled offices. Now they create an empty canyon of murky pools and green scum, their glass shattered, the abandoned shops and conference rooms filling with the soft susurration of the tide. Death lurks both above and beneath. Walls and floors can collapse, drowning you in stagnant water. Rusty edges hiding in the shallows, waiting to cut a bare, unsuspecting foot.

In the occupied district, the call to prayer crackles from a broken loudspeaker. A respite from the sharp-eyed snipers. The children breathe a collective sigh of relief. Nasser imagines he can hear the restless sea, whispering to him beyond the flooded towers. It's not just in his head, he realizes. He listens until he can make out the direction of the growing noise.

It isn't the sea. It's not coming from the rebels' camp either, or from the army positions, or from the vast slum on the hill where the town's survivors have gathered. This whisper rises from the direction of the beach. A big noise, like a brewing hurricane, only emanating from human mouths. It reaches him past the blighted highrises, the sunken compounds, and the last standing rows of tin-roofed shacks.

Someone hisses at him to stay down, but Nasser is already up and away. He vaults easily over the wall, then across to the next roof, seeking higher ground, until he has a view of the beach. Hidden behind an empty window, he spies on the commotion below the sunken tower. A long straggling crowd mills over the dirty sand – two trickles of people, one flowing downhill from the slum, the other joining it from the makeshift dwellings along the seafront creating a growing river of people heading for the sandbar south of the devastated town.

Perhaps another relief shipment in which case it pays to be the first in line. He takes the damp-gnawed steps two at a time, always faster than the others. They are scrambling after him, their shouts echoing along dark, empty concourses, half angry, half elated. Nasser laughs and sprints out into the sunlight, away from the stink of brine and rot, and onto the oil-soaked beach.

Fresh air rushes into his face and dries the sweat between his shoulder blades. Half a dozen steps, and the crowd swallows him, a torrent of noise and motion sweeping him along, carrying him toward the muddy swell of the sea. There are all kinds of people in it: round *mamas* who sell trinkets and food from stalls, cadaverous day laborers in ragged second-hand *calamidades* who squat in the dust and heat outside the Chinese office compounds looking for work, and shrieking children who chase each other between the feet of the throng. Gangs of teenage toughs cluster together, their affected scowls erased by childlike wonder. Nasser gives the thugs a wide berth, inhales the smells of sweat, sun-warmed skin, and dirt. He props himself up on his toes but can't see past the heads and shoulders of those ahead of him.

He tugs at sleeves and peppers those around him with questions but only receives glares and indifferent shrugs. Weaving in and out of the ragged procession, his impatient feet tap-dance on the hot sand until the figures part and he sees the object rising out of the waves in the shallows.

Gray froth surges around its vast bulk, the metal pitted and pocked and blackened from its passage through the heavens. It reminds Nasser of a beached whale from the old bootleg movies about the natural world, a seaborne giant long vanished into extinction. Only no whale, no living thing, has ever reached such extreme size. Its shape is that of a cigar smashed at both ends, easily the length of one of the highrises laid on its side.

Nasser sees the familiar UNFAR logo stenciled across the thing's center – except only the A and the R are still visible, but his mouth is already filling with saliva, stomach rumbling with hunger. It's an agrolander, a supply transporter from the orbital colonies. For a moment he's paralyzed. Then he breaks into a run toward the miracle, weaving through the crowd, feet churning up the surf, barely noticing the water as it slaps against his shins.

The sight of the soldiers brings Nasser to a halt. He's suddenly on his guard. The crowd closes its ranks around him and pushes him back further. Their murmur is a low, insistent noise on the verge of spilling into either fear or anger. "A gift from God," an old woman says, wiping tears from the crinkled corners of her eyes. "The jackals are already circling," says a tall laborer, wiry but muscular, glaring at the uniformed figures.

Even at a distance, Nasser can hear the tinny screech of the megaphone. Tatters of sentences make it to him despite the defective device, past the wind and the murmur of the throng.

Property of the people, the megaphone shrieks. *Warned... fair distribution... orderly manner.*

A truck is parked at the far end of the beach. Not an armored hulk, like the ones that guard the food banks and biotech crop fields, but a battered jalopy onto which someone has slapped an uneven coat of fresh green paint and an Army logo. An anti-aircraft machinegun from three wars ago and the skinny soldier manning it are supposed to lend some authority to the proceedings. Government troops have formed a shaky perimeter around the part of the spacecraft sticking out onto the beach. Standing under the blunt nose of the downed giant is the Special Commissar, waving the megaphone in front of his face. The Commissar is short and scrawny, barely old enough to shave. He looks slightly ridiculous in his oversized uniform and his boots filling with the sea.

Casemiro and the others arrive in a cloud of kicked-up sand and gaze at the scene in silent awe. Together with Nasser, they angle around the crowd for a better look while the Commissar recites a well-rehearsed speech about solidarity and hardship and shared responsibility. The situation is fully under control: a team of salvage technicians is already on the way from the capital. As soon as they arrive, the hatches on the beached agrolander will be opened, its contents logged, and appropriate shares distributed to the citizens.

The visible terror on the Commisar's face, the burden of unexpected responsibility, bely his officious tone. "Meanwhile," the Commissar says, "we declare this food shipment as the property of the people. It belongs to everyone equally. Anyone attempting to break inside will be considered a thief; a disaster profiteer stealing from his neighbor's mouth. Such a person will be punished accordingly. For the time being, it would behoove you to disperse and let us handle matters."

"Lies!" The accuser is a bent old man in a stained undershirt and shorts, purple scars showing under the white stubble of his scalp. He's standing back on the beach and addressing himself to those in his immediate vicinity, but loudly enough for everyone to hear him. "All lies! The Army will take the food for themselves. Or the politicians will take it. That's how it always works!"

A shudder of anger passes through the crowd, voices rising to jeer him, or hurl abuse at the soldiers. The Commissar ignores the old man, but a group of ruling party cadres scowl at him. "You'll shut up if you know what's good for you," the biggest among them says, the son of a local shopkeeper. The old man bows his head, but his eyes spark with defiance.

"When the hyena drinks, the dog can only look on," he says, loud enough to be overheard, drawing laughter from the crowd.

Tension builds in the heat, unfocused but easily directed at the first convenient target. There's a deep rumble of resentment beneath the jokes and laughter. Trouble is in the air. No famine relief convoys have come up the highway nor has any ship bearing provisions docked in the harbor in over a month. Driven by the promise of food, the crowd seethes and pushes forward, only a step or two for now, a thousand-footed creature testing its muscles. The soldiers raise their weapons hesitantly only then realizing they're outnumbered. A dozen paces or so and the crowd will force them into the sea.

"Comrades." The Commissar's voice crackles over the surly buzz of the crowd. "We are here to maintain order. I hear your concerns but there is no reason to worry. Maritime salvage rights grant us immediate ownership of any vessel, sea or space, floating onto the shores of our nation. This agrolander belongs to all of us."

"We should take whatever we can," says the old man, safely ensconced in a pocket of confederates, relishing the attention. "As soon as we can. Before these hyenas, or those other ones, come to eat their fill. Before they leave us with nothing."

"Nothing will be taken," says the Commissar, raising his arms in a calming gesture. "I urge you, brothers and sisters, to go to your homes. Give the engineers room to work when they arrive. There will be enough food for all."

To Nasser's astonishment, the young Commissar's words seem to sway the gathering. Many grumble and some shout insults but the mob's frenzy has dissipated. Nasser turns around and follows his friends across the sand, the sea erasing their footsteps.

"So much food." Casemiro glances back at the beached agrolander, his voice wistful. "How do they grow rice and beans in the sky? There are no fields in heaven."

"They make it with science, stupid." One of the other boys laughs, dodging away from Casemiro's kick aimed at his backside. Breathless with running and excitement, they join the rest of their group for the uphill trek in the garbage-strewn mud.

"I don't want any of you going down there," Mama says as she stirs dinner, waving the ladle she uses to dish out boiled *mandioca* to underscore her words. Her sermon is aimed at Nasser, but she makes sure to catch the eye of everyone seated at the table, shaven heads bowed over steaming bowls. "Every fool with a gun will be after that food. There will be shooting."

"Idiots." Assane chuckles, stirring *caril* sauce that isn't really *caril*, just a hash of reconstituted additives to give the starchy mess in their bowls taste and color. "All they'll do is get killed over it. The Army won't admit that the Armbands have already beaten them. They think the *azungu* will show up and open that thing for us, if only we ask them nicely."

"It didn't come from the azungu," Nasser says, "It came from up there. From space." He hadn't planned on speaking, but the words just came out.

"Listen to the brains of the family." Assane laughs unpleasantly.

"You go right ahead, little brother. Go down to the beach and wait. Go and stand with your hand out so the white man can lavish you with his generosity. Let the *azungu* take a photo of you. Maybe they'll put you on the cover of a magazine. Who knows? You might get an extra ration for looking so miserable."

Nasser spreads the mush across his bowl as a familiar sensation comes over him. It feels like the air has been sucked out of the room, like the space around him is shrinking, crushing his lungs. At nineteen, Assane has an opinion about everything under the sun, and most of those opinions are wrong. But try telling him that, and his hard, quick hands will cuff you on the back of the head before you can blink.

"It's a miracle," Mama says, glancing up, as if in prayer.

"The only miracle," Assane says, "is that the food conglomerates have not blown up the thing already to keep their prices high. It will also be a miracle if we get any of what's inside. Politicians are already drooling. A haul that size buys a lot of votes."

Mama waves Assane's tirade away. "All the same. No one in this house is catching a bullet. Is that clear?"

The boys murmur assent. Mama's eyes are on Nasser: he doesn't have to raise his eyes to know that. It's easier to lie if he doesn't meet her gaze. He flinches as the noise of a drunken fistfight erupts at the nearby *nipa* stand, right outside the too-thin walls of their shack. There are many empty stomachs in the *bairro* tonight, many eyes staring into the dark. If there's a chance to capture a chunk of the spoils, he'll have to take it soon.

Bairro Morro is a chaos of shacks and prefabs and tin sheet lean-tos, built from materials donated by the Chinese and the *azungu*, or salvaged from wrecked ships and flooded warehouses. Its squats and hovels groan under the weight of almost twenty thousand souls - a grasping, ever hungry horde with nowhere left to go.

When the house is silent and he feels like Mama's asleep behind the curtain partition, Nasser gets up and slips out the door, quiet as a ghost. He races down the pitch-black *ladeiras*, between sandbags and relief crates, over plastic Sanitas pipes, guided by muscle memory more than sight.

Casemiro is already there squatting behind the rough parapet. Down by the beach, the soldiers are exchanging sporadic long-range fire with the militants from the occupied district, who have grown bold under the cover of darkness. The boys peer over the wall to guess which side has the upper hand. But they quickly grow tired of the game and lie on their backs on a torn mattress watching the stars gleam through rents in the clouds. Dream of the treasures in the leviathan's belly: unimaginable delicacies and water purifying tablets, drugs that cure any disease overnight.

"It's magic rice," Nasser says, with an air of certainty. "Two grains in a pot, and you can feed your whole family."

"This one time we got GenPro pellets," Casemiro says. "They look like little balls of corn. But when you cook them, they taste like fish or chicken. Or *caril* with beans."

He reaches under the fraying collar of his shirt and pulls out an amulet on a leather thong. It's his *xicuembo*, which turns bullets to water or makes him invisible depending on the day. His Tia got it from a *curandeiro* in her village and has been protecting him ever since.

For a while, the two remaining boys are silent while they watch the beach. Blue flames flower around the black bulk of the agrolander. Techs with cutting torches move along the beach, hesitant at first, then encouraged by the absence of a response from the snipers.

"They're trying to cut it open," Nasser says, and laughs, more to release the tension than because he finds it amusing. "That will never work. They won't even scratch the plating. It's a waste of time."

But Casemiro doesn't take up the laugh. "When I get my share," he says, without looking away from the dark beach, "I'll trade it."

"You think they'll let us have any of it?"

"If not, we'll take it." There's that hardness in his friend's voice. Flat and determined and grown-up in a way Nasser can't quite put his finger on. They've all lost homes in the hurricane, but Casemiro has never had one, shuttled from one reluctant relative to the next for as long as he can remember. "We won't ask. We won't beg or wait for our turn to come. Just take what's ours by right. Then I'm leaving this place. I'm leaving it forever."

Leaving. Nasser feels like he's been punched in the stomach. "You don't know that there's anywhere else to go," he says, voice trembling. "Anywhere better than this. The Army is losing the war. Step out of town and the Green Armbands are everywhere. They'll kill you."

"Then they'll kill me." Casemiro turns to look at him, and Nasser takes an involuntary step back from the intensity in his friend's eyes. "But I'm not worried. My *xicuembo*, my amulet, will keep me safe."

Nasser has heard Assane and his friends brag about leaving whenever they take a few snorts of *nipa*. They talk about pipelines and deals and schemes to make them wealthy. But these are empty boasts. The *bairro* has a gravity of its own, one that does not obey the laws of physics. A gravity made of GenPro pellets in assorted flavors, of bags of Hi-Cal rice mix stamped with the UNFAR logo. Of the sounds of drunken violence outside and Mama crying softly after she turns off the lights. It pulls you into its orbit, and crushes you slowly, squeezing the life and dreams out of you, a long slog of hopeless days. That's all there is and all there will ever be. Death in thousands of tiny increments, waiting for the sea to rise higher and for the food assistance to stop coming.

Nasser could try to express all this. He could tell Casemiro how his own father had left, as had many of the fathers in town, only never to return. The world had gaped open to swallow him, an eternally hungry maw, grinding lives to dust. Out on the open water, or in the hellish confines of some illegal mine, deep in the bowels of the earth. But he doesn't say anything, only leans against his friend as they watch tracers streak the sky like meteors. Soon the boys drift away, under a cover of canvas and torn netting, sleeping the sleep of the exhausted and the hungry.

Dawn wakes them, and with it the shouting of voices and clamor of machinery below.

Nasser crawls out of their burrow and takes a long piss against the stripped-down remains of an excavator. Weak light filters down from the sky and the sun is barely an orange line over the water, but he can already feel its glare suck at the moisture inside him, drawing it out greedily, drop by drop.

He prods Casemiro with his foot until his friend groans and rolls over rubbing sleep out of his eyes. They survey the scene on the beach, but the figures are too far for them to work out what's happening. Agile as cats, they wend their way down the ruined access walkways. Down on the beach, they scrounge through a heap of discarded fruit, inured to the slime and stink of it, until they find a few pieces untouched by rot.

Alert for signs of danger, the boys slink along the edge of the beach, around stacks of worn-out car tires and looted shipping containers. With rising sun in his eyes, Nasser scans the armed figures deployed in a perimeter around the agrolander's nose. He takes a hissing breath and pulls Casemiro into cover as he makes out green armbands and bandanas. He's too far to read the inscription on the *braçadeiras*, but he knows it means *God*, in whose name so much blood has been spilled. Now he can see the corpses strewn across the sand.

"Government soldiers," Casemiro whispers. The militants stand over the corpses, scowling with rifles down across their chests. Most of them are young with wispy tendrils of the mandatory beards hanging off their chins and necks and sweat running down their smooth cheeks. A corpse drifts in the shallows and one of the militants is kicking it mechanically without much enthusiasm like a bored child.

Up on the back of the lander, saws scream and cutting torches hiss as the Green Armbands work to gain access through a sealed hatch. Scaffolding has been erected over its nose and a supply truck is parked on the asphalt strip by the wall. The militants are in high spirits. God has been merciful in sending them the means to continue the fight in His name. The riches inside the agrolander will rally more of the destitute to the Holy cause – starving villagers from the hurricane-stricken areas, willing to do anything in exchange for rations and medicine. A captain, or a commander, marches up and down the surf, screeching orders at the workers. Nasser feels the ground drop from beneath him. If the militants take the food, there will be nothing for the *bairro* residents at all. So far the spacecraft's thick hide has resisted the improvised machinery being pitted against it, but the rebels have plenty of time.

Fixated on the scene, he doesn't notice the shadow falling over him until it's too late. A rough hand shoves him down and a boot pins him to the hot sand.

Panicked, he tries to writhe free but the boot presses down mercilessly until he can barely breathe. He hears Casemiro make a surprised sound, then a dull smack as his friend lands on the ground next to him.

Two Armbands drag the boys closer to the lander and hold them at gunpoint as the Captain approaches who appears to be sweaty from shouting. Rivulets glisten in his thin beard, dark stains spreading under the armpits of his uniform. The Captain smiles, showing strong yellow teeth and mops his face with his sleeve.

"A gift from God," he says. The Captain is a thickset man with hard eyes, clad in a patchwork uniform. He brandishes an automatic rifle with a taped banana clip. With his free hand, he grabs Casemiro by the back of the neck and flings him into the circle of rebels.

"This one," the Captain says. "He's small enough. He looks quick. Send him up into the 'lander."

Guilty relief floods through Nasser followed by horror at what's happening. Now Casemiro seems to realize it too and starts struggling. The nearest militant backhands him across the mouth.

"Be careful." The Captain's cold shark eyes measure Nasser up and down. "Bring this one too. He might be too big to fit, but we'll find something for him to do."

A row of pilings, like the ones fishermen use to tie their boats, has been put up in the shallows. Nasser glances over and immediately regrets it. They're wooden stakes, and upon each a severed human head has been stuck. He thinks he can recognize the young Commissar and some of the soldiers, mouths agape above ragged, bloody stumped necks. Then another slap wrenches his head and he's already standing right under the leviathan, closer than he's ever been, gaping up at its immense scorched side.

"God is great," the Captain shouts from the beach. "You came here to steal. To rob the faithful before His eyes. Now you can redeem yourselves by doing His work instead."

A toolbox is thrust into Nasser's hands. Coils of cable are thrown over his shoulder. On numb legs, on feel that feel like they belong to someone else, he and Casemiro follow the Captain's barked commands, toward the militants' supply truck.

Hot sun beats down on the beach, stirring mirages from the sea and sand.

Delirious with hunger and thirst, Nasser looks up, his gaze drawn by a flash of sunlight on metal, far above the highrises. His feet tangle and he falls, dropping the tools he's carrying. A kick rouses him to his feet and he scrambles to retrieve his burden.

A groan of shredding metal comes from the top of the agrolander, followed by a collective cheer from the rebels. The Captain looks pleased. He motions for Casemiro to come forward.

"You know what to do," the Captain tells the boy. "Get inside. Find a way to open the door. Do it right and you both live."

From his belt, he retrieves a wicked-looking blade that shines bright in the midday sun. With unexpected swiftness, he steps behind Nasser, grabs the boy by the chin, and forces his head up to expose his throat. Before Nasser has the time to be afraid, he feels the sharp edge of the blade on his skin. A seasoned butcher, the Captain's touch is as light as a butterfly's kiss.

"If you don't, I'll cut your friend like a goat. Then I'll cut you. Then I'll head up there—" he points the knife at the slum atop the hill "-and slit the throats your mothers and fathers. If bastards like you two even have fathers. Do you understand?"

Nasser doesn't hear Casemiro's response, but the terrible force gripping his head releases him, and he slumps to the sand, rubbing his neck. Wherever he turns, he sees cruel, sweaty faces, rifles and machetes held menacingly. The Captain stands akimbo, a tiny, terrible god in his own tiny and equally terrible universe, demanding a blood sacrifice. There's no escape for Nasser. No pardon from this Hell.

Casemiro starts up the rickety scaffolding, his legs trembling visibly. Dark arms pull him up to the top, and he stands there for a moment, a small, miserable form outlined against the sky. In a quick movement, he disappears into the depths of the leviathan.

Minutes pass, then hours. Shadows grow long on the beach, bringing scant relief from the heat. Little by little, the rebels are slumping on their feet, exhausted by the night of fighting and the long, blazing day. The tide is coming in and the corpses bob in the surf, slowly drawn out to sea.

Birds circle above, sensing a feast. On the sandbar at the end of the blighted beach, a rebel lookout shields his eyes against the glare and fires a few warning shots in the air and yells something Nasser can't quite make out. Watchful of nervous trigger fingers, he looks for something to take cover behind, but the containers are too far and the men with guns too many.

A low whining carries across the water, and in a few moments a boat can be seen, heading directly in his direction. Still too far to make out a flag or a symbol. But it's an azungu boat with a powerful engine – an oil-burner, not one modified to run on sugar alcohol. Any child of the *bairro* would know that by the sound alone.

The boat's brazen approach sets off alarm bells in Nasser's mind. He remembers that flash between the clouds and suddenly feels very small and vulnerable under the open sky.

The militants have picked up on it too. The Captain issues curt orders and shoulders his rifle. The armed men stand on the sandbar with their rifles half raised as their ululations and shouts slowly give way to nervous silence. Nasser senses his moment to run, but the thought of Casemiro trapped in the leviathan's innards makes him feel like he's grown roots.

The boat has stopped and bobs on the waves outside the range of the *Braçadeiras'* weapons. A figure stands in the bow and raises a hand to its head.

Above the bay, something glints like glass, too quick for the eye to follow, scattering the squawking birds. Down on the beach, Nasser squints against the reflection of the sun on the water.

The flash strikes down from the sky so fast that its after-image sears itself into his retinas even as some instinct flings him facedown into the sand. White fire erases the sandbar. The rumble of the explosion almost lifts him back on his feet. If there are screams, they are swallowed as another missile strikes the beach, then another, until it feels like the earth is cracking open with the fury of the explosions.

Half-blind and deafened and nose bleeding, Nasser staggers up, weaving like a drunk. Falling back on all fours, he crawls into the shadow of the agrolander. He tries to make himself as small as possible.

Around him the sea froths red. Eviscerated shapes bump against his knees. A soundless scene unfurls as the caul clears from his eyes. The few surviving Armbands are scurrying across the beach trying to regroup and fire back at the attacking boat. But their attackers are in no hurry to call down another strike. They raise their own, longer-range weapons, and return fire. Nasser feels the thump-thump of bullets against the agrolander's hull, dropping one militant after another.

Death awaits him in the water, on the beach, and in the stretch of open space between him and the dubious safety of the shipping containers. Nasser flees up instead. He steps on something underwater that feels like a hand and pushes a floating bullet-riddled corpse aside with his foot. The scaffolding is miraculously still standing. He vaults up the bars and onto the top of the agrolander. Dropping down, he hugs the warm, abraded hull like a long-lost relative as bullets ping around him.

A hatch has been forced open, peeled back like the top of a can. Below, columns of smoke and dust rise from the explosion craters with bodies scattered around them like broken toys. A small hand reaches out from the warped hole of the hatch. Nasser seizes it and is dragged into the leviathan's belly.

Breath comes in gasps, panic galloping through his veins. His vision blurs as the darkness swallows him, his mouth as dry as sand. The dim space around him rings with the pounding of bullets on the hull. Casemiro clutches him, redolent of piss and terror, and Nasser clutches back, the two boys huddling in the darkness like moles hiding from the day.

A final burst of firing shakes the leviathan's bones, drowning out the screams of the injured and dying on the beach. The silence that follows is as sudden and frightening as the shots still ringing in their ears. Now the engine sounds closer and the boat's hull clangs against the siding; unintelligible voices drift into the airlock accompanied by the sound of feet. Nasser and Casemiro press themselves against the bulkhcads, as far away from the traitorous daylight shining into the hole as they can get.

But no one looks for them because no one expects two stowaway boys coming along for the ride. After a while, the engines kick over again, and metal shrieks and strains and grinds against the sand. Nasser yelps as a powerful shudder passes through the metal giant, toppling him backwards. He bashes his head against something hard and stars explode in the dark. Consciousness floats away down a dimensionless tunnel. By the time it fades back in, the floor beneath him is bouncing and dipping.

Even though he can't see what's happening outside, he senses the safety of solid ground falling away. He grabs Casemiro by the arm, pulls him out of the hatch, onto the spacecraft's reinforced hide.

Salt spray and wind lash the boys' faces. They are afloat on top of the leviathan. Behind them, the coast is receding, the *barrio* no more than a mound on the flat expanse of shore. Great black hawsers of carbon fiber bind the leviathan to the odd-looking boat, which moves with a slow and steady grace, tugging its oversized burden out to the open water.

Holding on for dear life, Nasser closes his eyes and screams. Over the wind and the sea, over the roar of the engines, a primal cry boiling up from the depths of his being.

The crew of the boat must have heard him because the vessel slows down, gradually, skillfully, until the ropes are slack, the huge shuttle lifting and dipping on the waves. A man stands up on the deck. Yells something in a language neither Nasser nor Casemiro can understand, but his authoritative tone is unmistakable.

When the boys hesitate, the man picks up his rifle and repeats his demand. Nasser and Casemiro don't think to disobey. Carefully, they make their way across the sun-warm hull of the agrolander towards the boat. Casemiro is crying silently but Nasser is too afraid for tears. A heavy and terrible knot of fear sits halfway between his throat and his stomach, turning his mouth as dry as the desert.

Standing over the boat, he sees it's full of soldiers. *Azungu* soldiers in unfamiliar uniforms, armed and body-armored. Their beefy upper arms sport red bands with a black symbol in a white circle, three sevens meeting in the center. Their rifles look shiny and new, almost unused, except Nasser has witnessed their destructive power firsthand.

Taking the wet, slippery hawser, he climbs down into the boat. The soldiers grab him and toss him to the middle of the deck where he is soon joined by Casemiro. Cruel eyes squint at them. The soldiers sneer and gibber in their alien, guttural tongue, laughing at the ragged castaways. Two or three of them are eating bars from shiny wrappers. In spite of his terror, in spite everything he's seen today, Nasser feels his stomach release a painful growl.

For a moment, the castaways are forgotten. The hawsers are cast off and the boat rumbles away, reducing the agrolander to a speck bobbing on the becalmed sea. A woman soldier with flaxen hair pulled into a tight bun holds up a tablet computer, her gloved fingers skimming quickly across its surface. Nasser thinks of the calories trapped inside the leviathan, of the thousands of hungry *barrio* mouths denied their meal.

The only warning he gets is the soldiers covering their eyes, clapping their hands over their ears. Nasser shoves his head between his knobby knees and tells Casemiro to do the same. "Open your mouth," he has time to tell his friend, thinking about the coming pressure wave, before the world explodes in another deafening roar.

Even at a distance, the shock rattles his insides, the concussive wave reaching across the water, shaking the boat like an angry dog with a rat. The soldiers whoop and laugh and clap their hands. Uncomprehending, Nasser looks up and sees the smoking wreck of the spacecraft sink into the bubbling waves. Tears course down his cheeks, which only increases the soldiers' glee.

Their job done, the *azungu* turn their attention back to the two castaways. A rangy, redheaded soldier winks at Nasser like it's all a joke. He cocks his finger back and makes a pistol. Nasser scans the faces around them and finds no compassion, no empathy, nor pity. Only a dull, piggish malevolence on the sunburned faces split by broad grins.

Maybe this is what Casemiro wanted, Nasser thinks, trying to control the tremor that rises from his core. Maybe this is their opportunity to leave. Maybe the soldiers will take them somewhere far away. Far from the *barrio's* oppressive gravity. But even as the thought crosses his mind, Nasser knows it's not true. He can try all he wants, but he's never going to leave that stretch of dirty beach, those ugly *favelas*. Like a ghost from old women's tales, he is cursed to haunt it. That other coast, the world beyond the infinity of water, will forever remain out of reach, a mirage shimmering under the terrible sun.

The soldiers join into the laughter, prod the boys with the hard tips of their boots. The redhead rolls his eyes and makes monkey noises at the boys. He makes exaggerated swimming gestures and jabs his finger at the coast, now a thin line on one side of the boat. Nasser holds his breath, tries not to let his horror paralyze his body. *Let us go*, he thinks, maybe even says out loud. Then the hands are on him again, lifting him like he weighs nothing at all.

For a moment he's suspended in mid-air, caught somewhere between the sea and the sky. They trade places and he hits the water hard, feels its cold, salty fingers reach into his nose and mouth.

Black panic unfurls across his thoughts but he tamps it down. To scream, to gasp for precious air, is to die. Instead, he turns his gaze up to the receding sun, spreads his arms to arrest his downward momentum and kicks his feet to reverse it.

He surfaces just as the soldiers are throwing Casemiro overboard. Nasser waits until he sees his friend's head pop up, spluttering and gasping for air. Already the sea is going to work on his undernourished muscles, cramping them up, coaxing them to give themselves over to the depths.

Laughter sails over the sound of the engines as the boat pulls away. An unwelcome image rises in Nasser's mind: he and Casemiro, two bits of driftwood in the immense blue. Panicked, he can no longer see the coast nor the hills. Only water.

A wavelet splashes his face, salty liquid in his eyes and nose. Nasser coughs and almost goes under as a result. He focuses on pushing the fear away. They haven't gone that far from the coast. He calms himself by finding the remains of the towers, the outline of Bairro Morro. He works out where the beach should be.

Nasser flips on his back and signals to Casemiro. His friend smiles through his fear and gives the thumbs-up sign. Casemiro is the best swimmer in their group, has been since the first time they jumped in off the old docks on a dare. He was diving like a fish before the others could muster up the courage to leave the shallows. Nasser knows they can make it. As long as he doesn't think about the distance ahead. As long as he doesn't let the leaden weight of futility overwhelm him.

Don't think up or down. Don't look behind. Not too fast, or too slow. One breath after the other.

He empties his mind and repeats the words like a mantra. Stretches his body and pumps his limbs, stiffly at first, then finding his rhythm. Digging and kicking in the direction of land.

Hours later, or what feels like hours, Nasser drags himself out of the surf. Wades out on all fours, almost falling into the huge furrow left behind by the towed agrolander. The waves are already working on filling it, and by tomorrow, all traces of the giant will be gone.

Nasser finds a spot on the sand beyond the grasp of the tide. He sits on the beach, waiting for Casemiro, long after the heavens fill with purple like spilled ink. After the stars come out to shine.

ON RAILS

A week before the train's last scheduled departure, Brody almost managed to get himself blown up.

His squad was crossing the grasslands in a wedge formation, sweeping the edge of the jungle. It wasn't a regular patrol, but a scheduled show of force, paid out of the Company's special initiatives fund: cerametal tactical vests and state-of-the-art rifles, an AI-guided satellite targeting system, sleek steel drones humming death from above.

Brody was dawdling along, soaking in the lush greenery and blue sky, thinking about how much the landscape resembled a scene from a movie, thinking about the cold beer at the end of his shift. Somehow he missed the tripwire and the guy behind him walked right into it. The grenade blew off the guy's leg below the knee just as trees erupted with firecracker noises. The pointman went down screaming and everyone else dove for cover. Brody flung himself into the grass and hugged the dirt as bullets streaked over him.

Within seconds, the AI had pinpointed the hostiles, painted them across the interior of his helmet's visor, and locked their positions into his smart sights. The squad regrouped, returned fire, followed up the bursts with white phosphorus grenades into the foliage. Brody let his rifle take over and sprayed the flaming figures that came shrieking and stumbling into the open, kept firing into the smoldering corpses long after they'd stopped moving.

It was over in less than seventy seconds, but it felt like a lifetime. No one was killed – the pointman's armor had done its job – but the episode left everyone shaken. It didn't matter that the rebels they were fighting were poorly trained subsistence farmers from the *llanos*, equipped with obsolete propellant firearms and bathtub explosives. They were equally apt to work as intended and blow the wielder's hands off. Time after time, the Company had been caught with its pants down, its three thousand troops and an armaments budget sufficient to arm a small nation notwithstanding.

They huddled in the open, in the midday heat, waiting for the all-clear from Home Base. Maitland eyed the booby-trap victim with a jaundiced eye. "That's one sure way out of this shithole," he said. "Full comp, paid recuperation leave. Do it myself, if I wasn't afraid of blowing my balls off."

It was Maitland's second tour in the *llanos*, and Brody had never asked the older man what had brought him here. Debt and poverty were the usual suspects, although lately he'd come to suspect that sociopathic violence ranked a close third. "I got a better way," he said. "Cushy seat fifty feet up in the air, cold drink in my hand. All expenses paid by the Firm."

"If you make it that long," Carlotti said.

"I'll make it," Brody said. "There's a month left on my contract. One week here, three in the MOB upcountry. Kicking my heels in an airconditioned rec room. Getting laid while you jerkoffs trade reacharounds after lights-out. Then home."

Carlotti sniggered, picked his teeth with his nail. "Keep telling yourself that, kid. You'll be back in the shit as soon as the money. Which will be sooner than you think."

"Our job is done here. They're closing the train depot."

Carlotti shot Maitland an exaggerated can-you-believe-this look. "You're asleep with your eyes open, pal. The Firm's been in the jungle six years. Winning hearts and changing minds. It'll be here another six, and the six after that. Protecting its mining interests. Except I've never seen any mines. Just the trees, and the fucking rebels in the trees."

"Give it a rest," Maitland said. He looked over at the lieutenant, who had raised his head and was staring at them.

"I'm serious." Carlotti lowered his voice, but not by much. "We pack up and leave here, we set up shop in some other part of this godforsaken shithole. Remember that when you're in line at the unemployment office this winter and it's negative twenty outside. The train goes everywhere, and we all ride it. Whether we know it or not."

"That was deep, Carlotti." The lieutenant came up to them, sweat streaming under his helmet. "Never figured you for such a philosopher. You hide it so well behind that hardscrabble trash exterior." He gestured at the stretcher on which the injured soldier lay grinning, high as a kite off his painkiller implants. "You and your friend Brody here get to haul this lucky bastard back to base. On foot, and on the double. Ought to give you some extra thinking time."

Ghost people fluttered in the trees. Gray silhouettes vanishing in and out of the shadows of the canopies, weaving through the undergrowth like smoke. To Brody's astonishment, there were entire tribes of them in the jungle, squat and black-haired, painted and tattooed in complex patterns. Heritage, affiliation, status: their skins were their ident cards, entire histories worn proudly on their chests and backs and limbs. It made no sense for anyone to still be living in the forest instead of following the money to the civilized areas, but hardly anything made sense in this hellish place.

Brody and Carlotti arrived with the stretcher a minute before the troop transport rolled in. The disembarking soldiers clapped ironically. Maitland handed Brody his water canteen. The three of them hung back behind the rest, walking slowly along the fence that separated the base from the depot. A battered train was sitting on the tracks, a tattered metal snake basking in the sunlight, reeking of oil and soot, even at a distance. Past the depot, where the forest began, Brody could see the tribesfolk gathering. They couldn't all be looking at him, but he felt their scrutiny as a prickling on his sweaty skin. He could never get rid of the sense of being watched, not in his bunk, not on the john. Like the jungle, that green inferno, had itself grown eyes.

"Savages," Maitland said, following Brody's look across the fence. He spoke with something akin to admiration. "They live off the forest. Hunt, pick, dig up roots. They haven't yet been *saved* by civilization."

"Why don't they leave?" Brody knew better than to ask questions, but sometimes words just tumbled out of his mouth, bypassing his brain. "There's got to be better places than this."

Maitland smoked his Electric Blues, peppermint-scented vape that he claimed helped keep away the bugs. "It's their land," he said. "The Firm's been trying for years. Lots of money to be made from it. But the tribes won't budge."

He took a drag and blew a perfect smoke ring. "They believe their ancestral spirits are here, or some bullshit. You know how it is with primitives and their superstitions."

"But we're doing it anyway," Brody said. Every few weeks or so, another group of ghost people would be rendered homeless by the bulldozers, escorted out of the clearance zone, to the collection barracks. "Isn't that what the train is for?"

"We're trying to civilize them," Carlotti said. It sounded rote, a repetition of something he didn't quite understand. "Put shoes on their feet and get the lice out of their hair. Send them off to work in the cities. The Firm teaches them skills other than hunting and fishing and screwing, helps them make something of themselves. That's the whole point."

"So much for forest spirits." Brody grunted, ground his own cigarette out underfoot. "If they were any good, the natives would be the ones winning."

There's no winning against the Firm," Maitland said. "They got deep pockets and an endless supply of unemployed yahoos ready to carry a gun for them. If we all get killed today, we'll be replaced tomorrow. You either ride the wave, or you get crushed. That's all there is to it."

The three men went silent and watched the most recent batch of natives, scrubbed and dressed in shapeless, identical clothing, file into the depot from the barracks. A man in a business suit walked along the long lines of people calling out names and numbers off a list.

Brody took a hit off Maitland's vape and watched the smoke drift over the depot. Back when he'd signed up, the motivation had been clear. *This is my war. This is what I'm fighting for. To never come back to this place.* But everywhere he'd gone with the Firm, things had been the same. Flooded coastal cities, skies black with the soot of continent-sized forest fires, endless rows of disheveled and dispossessed refugees. Was this the world he'd been persuaded to fight for?

"Have you ever been to one of the Institute's centers?" he asked as the train doors closed and the engine clattered to life.

"What centers?" Carlotti said.

Brody pointed at the huge billboard above the train platform. THE TRENCHARD INSTITUTE, the letters read. WHERE HUMAN POTENTIAL BECOMES HUMAN ADVANCEMENT.

Maitland's mouth twisted in a suspicious grimace, but he said nothing. Carlotti shook his head. "No. They're up north, right? In the cities?"

"That's what they tell us," Maitland said. "Natives go up to the centers to get educated. Natives come back after the farms have been built. The Firm gives them schools, streets, malls, roads. Everyone wins."

"Fine by me," Carlotti said, nodding.

"You see any schools being built around here?" Maitland asked him.

"Like it matters what happens to a bunch of shit-caked savages," Carlotti said, rolling his eyes. "The Company takes care of us, we take care of business. Natives getting on that train is part of the business. That's all I need to know."

"We don't wear logos," Brody said. He glanced over at his comrades' uniform shoulder straps. The wheels in his head were starting to turn, a little rusty, but gaining momentum.

"What the fuck does that have to do with anything?" Carlotti turned to him with a frown.

"No logos. No insignia." Brody spoke slowly, thinking, trying to articulate the elusive connection. "That's normally the first thing a corporation does. Put up a sign. Stake a claim. Every beer shack in town has at least two or three. But we don't. We just get picked up at the MOB and airdropped in the middle of the night, into a fully equipped base that's not marked on any map. It's like we're trying to stay invisible. That sound normal to you?"

Carlotti sighed and shook his head in exasperation. "Yes, Brody. That sounds pretty normal to me. I get paid to carry a gun and point it at people my employer wants me to point it at. Sometimes to pull the trigger. I'll leave the thinking to the assholes with MBAs."

"Right." Maitland's gaze met Brody's and held it. Something like understanding passed between them – at least Brody felt it. "Don't ask questions above our pay grade. Keep your head down and do your job. Cash the paycheck. That's all there is to it."

The town by the base was an ugly pile of tin shacks and low concrete prefabs, scattered through the valley in a rough approximation of urban planning. One of the temporary settlements that sprouted in the wake of the Company's relentless march into the interior, it was already showing symptoms of its impending demise: abandoned shops, cracks in the walls, drug addicts sprawled in the ditches.

The day before the last transport, the trio walked into a bar that doubled as a brothel, a two welded-together cargo containers with broken neon signs blinking from its corrugated roof. Inside was cheap beer and the same handful of overworked whores. A new shift had come in on the train and the peeling counter was packed with drunk, bored corporate personnel. Couples swayed in the center of the dirty linoleum floor, sloppily pawing each other to the appalling electro-beat from the tinny speakers.

Carlotti liberated a section of the bar with his elbows and ordered beers. Reaching into the pocket of his civvies, he held up a small plastic bag with a leer. "Got these on Tuesday with my personal shipment," he said, flicking the pink pills inside. "My cousin says they're the big thing up in the Sprawl. All the white collar types pop them like they're going out of style."

"Good for them," Brody said, indifferent. He swigged his beer, finding no pleasure in the watery, lukewarm taste. Either as a joke, or from some misguided attempt to decorate, the greasy walls were covered in old Trenchard posters. The blank-feral faces on the poster in front of him saw to that, a comically exaggerated lenticular image of natives before and after reeducation. Naked savages with spears and skins in the jungle gave way to plump peasants before fields of amber grain. TRENCHARD INSTITUTE, the tagline proclaimed. THINKING IS MAN'S GREATEST VIRTUE.

Carlotti wagged a finger at him. "Cut that crap, Brody. You're even uglier when you're trying to think. Anyone ever tell you that? I didn't think it was possible either, but here I am, proven wrong. We're here to have fun, okay? Not to look at your mopey mug."

Brody drank more of his beer, flipped Carlotti the bird. "Thinking is man's greatest virtue. Says so right in the Company manual."

"What?"

"Nothing." Brody set his bottle on the sticky bar. He was suddenly sick of it all, physically sick and morose, as if all blood had curdled in his veins. "We're not paid to think, right? If you ever feel like thinking, the Firm's got just the right answer. Drop a tab and check out. That's the easy way." He kept thinking to the natives, washed and dressed in company cast-oofs, boarding the train. Then to the cordoned zone he'd grown up in, the unemployment lines and food kitchens, the constant rage and despair.

"Damn," Carlotti said. "Who pissed in your cornflakes?"

Brody peeled the label off his beer bottle. "What did you mean back there?" he said to Maitland. "At the depot. When you said that thing about the training centers."

"Not that shit again." Carlotti pleaded to the ceiling.

"Nothing." Maitland was facing the dancers. His beer was already gone: he signaled for another. "Just that the centers are supposed to be north. Near the big hubs. But the rail line goes east to west. Deeper into the jungle."

"None of it makes sense," Brody said. He thought back to his enlistment. *Profit knows no ideology*, the corporate spin doctor at the recruitment center had said. *We're creating a new reality, a rational one. A vast tide of progress that will lift all boats.* "The Institute spends all this time and money educating savages. Turning them into clerks, or waiters, or whatever. Cheap labor for the local companies, but how much can they earn back on them? What's the profit incentive?"

"Jesus." Maitland pounded the bar with his palm, shouted at the bartender to hurry up. "It's like a zoo in here. Can't hear myself think over those shitty speakers."

"It's always the same train," Brody continued. "Also, why do they need that many compartments? They never take more than a few hundred natives at a time."

Maitland looked at Brody out of the corner of his eye. His mouth worked as if he wanted to speak, but he looked away again. "You'll drive yourself crazy, thinking like that," he said at last. "In a week or two, it'll be someone else's problem. You and I, we're just hired meat. Don't rock the boat. Nothing good can come of it."

Brody nodded slowly. He gazed down the bar and saw a group of transportation techs passing out drinks to a bunch of whores. "Maybe those guys can tell us," he said, pointing with his head. "Carlotti, you still got those pills from your cousin?"

"Yes, and I'm not sharing anymore." Carlotti put a protective hand over his pocket. "You're shitty company, Brody. So shitty you almost make Maitland seem fun in comparison. That's how bad you are. You may want to do something about that."

"How about we take a look for ourselves," Brody said. He held Maitland's gaze until the older soldier gave a barely perceptible nod. Carlotti groaned, outnumbered. "I'm going in. You two can do what you want."

He was off his stool and pushing through the hot, sticky bodies, unsure what he was doing, or was about to do. Behind him Carlotti was shouting something, but it was swallowed by the noise of the bar, by the screeching music.

Two of the techs were leaning on the counter, the others gyrating with the girls on the dance floor. Brody sidled in next to them, caught the nearest one's eyes, then smiled. The tech was young and scrawny, sweating in his overalls. His grin indicated that he was already three sheets to the wind. The other one was stout and red-faced from the heat, swaying on his stool.

"How's it going?" Brody yelled over the music. "You fellas look familiar. Have I seen you here before?"

"Not here," the skinny tech said. "We rotate every four weeks. That's the policy."

Brody signaled beers all round. "You must have come on the last train. Are you guys staying a while?"

The skinny tech shook his head, gulped down the beer. "Just forty-eight hours. We head back the day after tomorrow." He grinned at a thin whore who was waving at him from the crowd. "Quick turnaround this time. It's our last gig in this camp."

Brody acted surprised. "Man, they sure keep you guys busy. Back and forth between the camps and the education centers, week in, week out."

"What?" The boy's unfocused eyes narrowed, then widened. He threw his head back and laughed, as if Brody had told a joke. "Right. The education centers. There's so many of them, I lose track sometimes."

The fat tech glared past his buddy and right at Brody. "Hey," he said, clamping a meaty hand on his comrade's shoulder. "If you can't hold your booze, keep your trap shut."

Brody propped his elbow on the bar and swayed drunkenly. "Hey, can a guy grab a lift on the train? I've been wanting to see the coast for ages. Maybe when my next leave comes up?"

The fat tech was eyeing him suspiciously. "No can do, man. The Company's got a strict policy against free riders. Sorry."

Brody shrugged. He saw Carlotti pass the pill bag to Maitland under the counter. "S'okay. At least you get to see the sights. Beats having your ass shot at and getting stung by bugs. I'd kill to have your job."

The techs exchanged a wary glance. "It ain't all it's talked up to be," the younger one said, looking subdued. "We just do what we're told."

"No argument from me on that, buddy," Brody said, taking two fresh bottles from Maitland. "Hey, how about another round?"

The depot was empty, only a few lights struggling in the black of night. None of the checkpoints were manned, and no one stopped the three soldiers from using the techs' ident cards on the automated gates.

"Your cousin wasn't shitting you," Maitland said to Carlotti as they climbed up to the platform. "I hope those boys don't have to be anywhere early in the morning."

Carlotti wasn't amused. "Once we go in there," he said, gesturing at the train, "we've crossed a line. There's no going back. Do you two assholes understand that? Whatever there is to know, we'll know."

"Thank you for explaining that," Brody said, far more breezily than he felt. "Never would have worked it out myself. The lieutenant was right. There's real brains behind that inbred squint of yours."

The train was right by the platform, closer than ever. Its rear cars sported tinted windows, but the forward ones had none, only a scuffed metal strip along the middle. The three soldiers entered the passenger car almost unobserved. The duty tech shot them a resentful glance, then lowered his dataglasses and went back to his streaming. Brody froze, but Maitland walked past without a word.

"These guys don't know each other by face," he said in a whisper as they made their way down the aisle. "We'll probably be on some security camera somewhere, but there's no reason for anyone to check the footage."

"Why would anyone be checking footage?"

"No idea," Maitland said. "But there's got to be a reason for all the hush-hush. You saw those two clowns at the bar. Dead drunk, both of them, but they wouldn't say a word about what goes on here."

But there was nothing unusual about the passenger car, or the ones after it. Only neat rows of seats, a little worn, and wide windows giving onto the silent platform. Brody's skin crawled with tension, his nerves screaming at him to get out. Maybe his gut feeling was wrong. Maybe it was just a train like any other. If he hurried back to the dorms, he could still catch a few hours of shuteye before another sweltering, backbreaking day.

Carlotti was looking increasingly nervous. "Alright," he said, glancing over his shoulder at the door between the cars. "We came, we checked things out. Everything's fine. Time to get out of here."

Brody leaned over the seats, stared out the window. "How many do you reckon went on the train last time?" he said. "Two hundred? Two fifty?"

"I don't think quite two hundred," Maitland said.

"That sounds about right," Brody said. "There's around two hundred seats in this car alone. Give or take a dozen. Also, these windows are one-way glass. You can see out, but no one can see in."

"Meaning what?"

"Meaning why have all the other cars? I'm no business genius, but running a train of empty cars sounds like a piss-poor way to make money." Brody pointed down the aisle. "Meaning there's something in those other cars the bosses don't want us to see."

They reached the end of their car. Brody studied the door. Unlike the rickety affair through which they'd entered, this one was massive and solid steel. Next to the handle was an ident scanner. He tapped his chin with the pilfered ident card, turned to his comrades. "We'll go through this door," he said, "and find another car, just like this one. Nothing remarkable about it."

"Nothing." Maitland nodded in agreement. In the harsh lights of the train, his face was very pale, unsmiling. "Then we leave."

"We can go back to the bar," Carlotti said, swallowing hard. "Drink our faces off and have the worst hangover tomorrow. We won't remember any of this."

Before he could talk himself out of it, he pressed the ident card to the plate. The backlight went on, then turned green, and the door slid open.

Breath whooshed out of Brody's lungs, air he had not realized he'd been holding.

The space beyond was bare and almost blindingly white. It smelled strongly of antiseptic and something unfamiliar, offensively chemical. Neon tubes flickered on as they pushed through a turnstile. A simple plastic desk with a built-in console stood to the right. To the left, flush against the walls, were big wheeled laundry hampers.

At the far end was another door. This one was closed with a bulky metal wheel and thick rubber around the frame.

"Okay." Maitland's voice was weak with relief. "Okay. We've seen what there is to see. Now let's get out of here before someone finds us."

Brody rolled one of the hampers aside and tapped the wall. "Solid," he said, looking up and down the riveted seam in the train wall. "But from the outside, we saw see a row of windows. Just like on all the other cars." The full picture still evaded him, but the implications made the hairs on the back of his neck stand up.

"We could be wrong about that," Maitland said, looking around like a trapped animal. "Maybe we got turned around."

"This is wrong." Carlotti went back to the turnstile, came back shaking his head. "None of it makes sense."

Brody went over to the console, touched the ident card to the terminal. "Locked," he said. "I don't suppose either of you asked those techs for a password."

They gathered by the sealed door, tried one ident card, then the other, then both at the same time. The reader flashed red and the door stayed closed. But even without going in, all three men had seen the biohazard symbol above it, and it didn't take a leap of imagination to work out what happened in there.

"Listen." Carlotti licked his lips, spoke through a throat suddenly constricted by fear. "Listen. We can't stay here. We weren't meant to see this. If we leave, maybe we'll get away with docked pay. Maybe we'll be fired. But if we stay—"

"Tomorrow they'll open the doors," Brody said. "People are going to get on. Real living people, who'll never get off." *Like everyone back home*, the thought came to him. Choking on poisoned air, scrabbling like hungry rats in a maze. *Like us over here.* "That's the better life we're setting them up for, boys."

Cold horror shuddered through Brody as he realized he was part of it. One tiny cog, turning, blind to its role, but no less guilty for its ignorance. "Maybe they're savages," he said, in a voice that sounded like someone else's. "Maybe we think they live like animals. But they don't deserve what we're doing to them."

"Shut up, Brody." Carlotti's voice was a strained whisper. "Shut the hell up, or I swear—"

"Hey."

The three soldiers turned to see the duty tech in the doorway, scowling at them. "You clowns aren't authorized to be here after hours," the tech said, still half distracted into his streaming. "It's a restricted area, and I haven't received a maintenance ticket."

Brody and Carlotti stood frozen, ident cards outstretched toward the scanner. Maitland swallowed, broke the silence. "System must have glitched again," he said, shaking his head. "We can't get in." As he spoke, he was making his way across the aisle, shoulders slouched, unthreatening.

"Get in?"

"Maybe you could help us out." Self-conscious grin in place, Maitland spread his arms helplessly. Closed the distance between them by a few more steps. "Do us a solid? It's the middle of the night, and we'd really appreciate some sleep. We got a malfunction report. Probably nothing. Another ghost in the machine. But if we don't get it fixed, we'll be stuck here until morning. How about you open the door for us?"

"Open the door?" The tech drowsily gaped from one man to the other. Then his gaze sharpened and he straightened up. "That's a Code Red compartment. Where the hell are your suits? I'm calling this in."

He turned to go, but Maitland was on him in two bounds, grabbing him under one arm and by the back of the neck, slamming him face-first into the doorframe. Nose broken, the tech let out a gurgling squawk, more of surprise than pain. Brody rushed forward. Maitland was still holding his victim, who was battered, but conscious.

Escape, Brody thought, with a frantic glance at the exit doors. "Get up," he said to the tech. "You're going to walk us out. Kill the surveillance." What then? He couldn't think that far ahead. In his mind's eye, he saw the jungle, a maze of dark paths vanishing into dew-beaded leaves. That way was life. *Freedom.*

"I can't," the tech said in a thick, nasal voice. He coughed, hawked, spat out a dark red gob. "I don't have the codes. I'm just the night guy." His wide, panicked eyes flicked between the three soldiers. "I won't tell. I swear."

"Why do we need suits to go in there?" Carlotti said, jabbing his finger at the door. "What's Code Red?"

The tech gave him an incredulous look. "Nobody goes in without a suit and portable air supply," he said. "Because of what's in there. Are you nuts? Nobody."

"Nobody?" Maitland said through clenched teeth. His hands were squeezed into fists on the tech's uniform collar, knuckles white. "You sure? Nobody goes in without a suit?"

"Well." The tech hesitated. "No one except the, you know. But it's all right. It's quick. They don't feel a thing. We tell them it's a sanitation thing. Hell, for the Company, it sort of *is* a sanitation thing, right?"

Jumbled visions clouded Brody's head. Of about his father, his wheezing lungs and trembling hands, standing outside the gate of the shut-down plant. Of his mother, smiling a wan smile down on him as they stood in the line for the soup kitchen. No corporate benefit plan for those two, only the sterile, impersonal embrace of the euthanasia clinic. Of the men and women and children who would file through the train doors in the morning, eager to begin their journey.

He was distantly aware of Maitland shouting at him, of Carlotti making a half-hearted grab at him, of a cold metal weight in his hands. Aware of his muscles pumping, swinging the weight up and down, driving it into the prone thing on the floor. Feeling the impact, a hard crunch at first, then softer, warm and pulpy.

He blinked. The fire extinguisher rolled out of his hands. He smelled the coppery scent of blood on his hands, his clothes, pooling on the floor. "That's enough," Maitland said, holding him back. He said it over and over, like a prayer.

"Fuck. Oh, fuck." Carlotti had backed himself up against a wall, eyes closed, as if trying to wake up. "You killed him. What do we do now?"

"We can't stay here," Maitland said, pulling Brody up. "We got to run. Clean ourselves up and go. Get over the hills, try for one of the villages on the other side. Maybe we can make it there by morning."

The door behind the dead tech swished open. Armored figures were advancing into the car, crouched behind riot shields. Maitland froze in place, started to spread his hands, but a bright blue arc snapped across his chest before he could move a muscle. He twitched, spun, and crashed heavily against the seats. A second crackle a moment later, and Carlotti crumpled to the floor, convulsing so hard Brody heard his teeth crack.

Swaying, Brody tried to focus his gaze on the visored helmets. *It's okay*, he wanted to say. *We're not going anywhere. Don't you see? For people like us, the train is all there ever is.* But what came out of his mouth instead was the song of the jungle: the screams of birds, the roar of the nearly-extinct jaguar, the patter of rain on glossy green leaves.

The taser came up, electricity sparked at the muzzle, and the thought fled his mind, driven away by darkness.

A vast voice boomed out from above, shattering the gloom, stirring the stifling air. The words were distorted, a deep vibration in the ground, but Brody understood the message.

It was time to go.

He stepped obediently in line with the others, a long row of them, stretching from the barracks to the platform. Sensation washed over him: the shadows inside the building, then the sudden, shocking transition into daylight, the guards and the wire fence, the smell of sweat and disinfectant and something else, like freshly turned soil. But below that, below the register of direct impressions, lay only darkness, cool and featureless. He didn't mind that. It was easier this way – to put one foot after the other, to go where the men with the guns pointed.

Across the yard, then up the platform.

The train stretched the entire length of the station, its shiny track disappearing into the leafy verdure. Oval windows scintillated with sunlight, threw back his own reflection. Shorn-headed and hollow-eyed, the barely healed scar on his right temple twisting his entire face out of true. Suddenly he felt afraid. A dark and awful awareness bubbled under the chemical sludge coating his thoughts. He whimpered and tried to turn back, but other bodies pressed into him, pushing him closer to the opening doors.

As soon as he stepped on the train, the moment of terror passed, replaced by glacial calm. A train meant a journey. It meant the sights and smells of faraway places. Placated, he stepped into the cool interior, lowered himself into a seat.

A young woman smiled at him. Small and round-faced, like his fellow passengers, she cradled a small child in her arms. The child's mouth was open in a yawn, or a cry, one chubby hand reaching up. Brody smiled back. It felt good to smile, and he hadn't been doing much of it lately. The white coats had changed that. They had reached inside his head and taken his dark thoughts away. Now the world was a bright, simple place again, hot sun and blue skies and the breathtaking green of the forest, stretching forever, to the very edge of the earth.

Glancing over his shoulder, he scooted into the empty seat by the window. Other passengers were settling in around him, seats creaking in near-complete silence. Soon the doors would close and they would be off. A train meant change: there was enough left of him to acknowledge this basic truth.

When the platform started to inch away from him, slow at first, then faster, Brody leaned closer to the glass and drank in the sight of the jungle unfolding outside the windows, the trees arching overhead, as if whispering secrets only he could hear.

Damir is the author of the novels *Kill Zone* and *Always Beside You*, and short stories featured in multiple horror and speculative fiction magazines and anthologies.

An auditor by trade and traveler by heart, he does his best writing on cruise ships, thirty-plus thousand feet in the air, and in the terminals of far-flung airports.

He lives in Virginia with his wife. When not writing fiction, he reviews horror movies, discusses books, and shares his unsolicited opinions on just about everything on his blog, Darker Realities.

Contact the author or read the full bio on thmaduco.org:

For any related live events or collaborations, please contact The Mad Duck Coalition through its contact form.

Author Recommendations

Paolo Bacigalupi
The Windup Girl

Bruce Sterling
Islands in the Net

John Joseph Adams and Hugh Howey
The End is Nigh

Ian McDonald
Luna: New Moon

Kim Stanley Robinson
Red Mars

And the special works of his fellow
mad ducks.

Concluding Note

Thank you so much for purchasing this work! Your support allows us to continue to avoid resorting to anti-consumer DRM practices and encourages our authors, not just this one, to continue following their passions and producing intellectually stimulating works. It also enables us to provide special programs for supporters like you!

One of our programs is a special discount for reviews, positive and negative! We believe that even negative feedback is vital feedback, so you should say what you really think. For more information about our review program, contact us through our contact form and select the appropriate category. In short, if the thought of supporting the authors and our jolly little coalition isn't enough to move you, we offer 5% off your next order for each review you post, with limitations obviously. So send us a message!

Information about our other programs and offers can be found on our website, including but not limited to: complimentary copies, contests, and collaborations.

Please reach out for further information. If you couldn't tell, we like to...quack!!!

The Mad Duck Coalition

The Mad Duck Coalition publishing house is a group of innovative intellectuals who want to publish what they are passionate about without compromising themselves or their work solely in the hopes of being published.

As such, The MDC publishes quality works that intellectually stimulate the mind, not necessarily the pockets. We wholeheartedly believe that quality and commerciality are two different things and that quality is far more important.

Check us out at
thmaduco.org: